Other books by Jane McBride Choate:

Think of Me
Convincing David
Heartsong Lullaby
Never Too Late for Christmas
Mile-High Love
Cheyenne's Warrior Rainbow
Desert Paintbox

WOLF'S EYE

WOLF'S EYE

•

Jane McBride Choate

AVALON BOOKS

NEW YORK

Published by Thomas Bouregy & Co., Inc.
160 Madison Avenue, New York, NY 10016

Library of Congress Cataloging-in-Publication Data

Choate, Jane McBride.
   Wolf's eye / Jane McBride Choate
      p. cm.
   ISBN 0-8034-9765-2 (hardcover : alk. paper)
1. Women ranchers—Fiction. I. Title.

PS3553.H575W65 2006
813'.54—dc22

2005033847

PRINTED IN THE UNITED STATES OF AMERICA
ON ACID-FREE PAPER
BY HADDON CRAFTSMEN, BLOOMSBURG, PENNSYLVANIA

To Marilyn, the two Marys, Darlene, and Grace
who never stopped believing in me.

Prologue

Rebecca Whitefeather worked feverishly over the sheep, trying to save it even while knowing that the task was futile. The misery in the animal's eyes confirmed her own diagnosis.

The night deepened around her, the wind picking up, the air chilling as she worked in the open field. Her hands turned icy as she labored over the animal. A shudder, born more of pity than weariness, trembled through her.

Finally, she stood. She bowed her head, praying for the strength to do what needed to be done. A deep breath later, she was ready.

She prepared the euthanizing needle and injected the animal. No rancher enjoyed having to put an animal down, but it was kinder than allowing the poor beast to suffer.

It was done. Only now did her knees threaten to buckle. She huddled deeper in her jacket against the coldness of the Colorado night as well as that inside her own heart.

A coil of pain spiked, then settled deep in her chest. She tamped it down. A soft heart wasn't an asset when it came to ranching. Tears crowded behind her eyes and threatened to spill over so that she had to hold her head up to prevent it.

She knew that Uncle Ray would have spared her the task, but she would never have asked it of him. She, alone, was responsible.

Her knees were no longer weak, and the horror she felt was slowly being replaced by anger. That most of that anger was directed at herself didn't lessen its sting.

It had been she who had steadfastly refused to set traps for the wolves that raided her flocks. Even now, she couldn't bear the thought of using the cruel traps.

Wolves. The stuff of legend and fable. And now a deadly menace. Their natural prey had all but disappeared, so they'd taken to raiding the ranches and farms for food.

The ranchers had banded together to eliminate the predators. She didn't blame them. The wolves threatened the livelihood, not just of the ranchers, but of all those who did business with them.

Wolves, so wild and beautiful and free, were a danger to the ranchers . . . and to themselves. A stab of sadness cut through her.

Silently, Uncle Ray loaded the carcass on the truck. "I'll see to it."

She nodded, unable to summon the energy for words.

A heavy hand cupped her shoulder. "You showed strength tonight. Your ancestors would be proud."

Rebecca found that she could smile after all. Uncle Ray, actually her great-uncle, was the one constant in her life. He had taken care of her when her parents had died twenty years ago in a car accident.

Uncle Ray had lost his wife, her father's aunt, in the same accident. It seemed right that he should move in with her and take care of her.

The land was in her name. It had belonged to her mother. Her father, a full-blooded Navajo, had married the pretty daughter of a local rancher.

In the Navajo way, Rebecca didn't believe that she owned the land. She held it in trust, a steward to care for it, nourish it, protect it. Now she was in danger of losing it.

The land was her heritage, her link to the past, her passport to the future. She had plowed whatever extra money she had—and there was precious little—back into the land.

Too little money and too little time. A rancher's lament.

She was tired, she thought, worn down and worn out,

like a horse rode hard and put away wet. Absently she rubbed the back of her neck. The pain there was pretty much constant these days, the sort of ache brought on by too much worry and not enough of everything else.

Chapter One

Rebecca watched the black wolf bound away, then turn and pause, as though taunting her with his latest exploit. Her fingers gripped the butt of her rifle, but she couldn't pull the trigger. Even after Uncle Ray had buried a sheep two nights ago, she couldn't bring herself to destroy the animal.

For the second time in as many days, she felt weak, an emotion she detested.

She let her gaze linger on the wolf, taking in its proud bearing, flared nostrils, shiny coat so dark that it appeared black against the sun-bleached landscape.

Placing fresh meat around the perimeter of the meadow had been her idea. The wolf had taken the bait and still managed to escape the snares Rebecca and her men had set.

She stared in reluctant admiration at the beautiful animal. She'd named it Santanna the first time she'd seen it.

She knew this bold marauder almost as well as she knew herself. They were old enemies and old friends. The inconsistency didn't bother her. She respected Santanna, just as she would respect any man . . . or animal . . . who fought for what was his.

Instinctively Santanna, the leader of the pack, knew where Rebecca had chosen to graze her flock and where to look for water. He knew how to find shelter from the harsh winds that blew undeterred across the high plains of southern Colorado.

He was a master of escaping the scores of men who'd tried to put a bullet in his hide or capture him in a steel trap. Many a time, a rancher had followed Santanna into what appeared a box canyon, only to find that the wolf had an escape route.

Rebecca had never been among those who tried to capture Santanna. She'd listened to the stories of men who'd matched wits with the wolf and had secretly cheered Santanna's escapes. She valued her own freedom too much to deprive it from anything so untamed as the big wolf.

Until now.

Santanna had crossed the line. He'd taken Rebecca's sheep one time too many, her passport to making her dream come true.

"You've gone too far this time, my friend," Rebecca said, the softness in her voice at odds with the hard look in her eyes. "Why didn't you stay where you belong?"

The question was a rhetorical one. She knew the answer as well as she knew there wasn't an answer. The drought had driven wolves closer to civilization where they raided the ranches and farms. Drought meant fewer prey, more competition for what there was.

Rebecca knew she wouldn't get another chance, not today. The wolf was too cunning to be taken in again. Even now, the animal raised its head and pricked his ears, sensing danger.

Santanna had beaten them. For today. There'd be another time, Rebecca promised.

She swept off her hat, a silent salute to the victor, and then replaced it. She didn't delude herself that it would be easy to capture the wolf or the pack of predators he lead. Nor did she want to.

Santanna belonged to the land as surely as did the wind, but he wasn't leaving her any choice.

Rebecca knew some of the ranchers used steel traps. She had held fast against the cruel snares. Any living thing, even the predators who were destroying her livelihood, deserved better than that. She'd seen animals who had chewed off their legs in an attempt to free themselves.

The pounding of hooves pummeling the drought-hardened ground had her turning in her saddle. She watched as two of her men rode up. They wore the same rueful expressions which she knew shadowed her own face.

"Sorry, boss," Ben Hooper said, taking off his hat and wiping his forehead with a sweat-stained kerchief. "He's a wily devil."

"That he is." Rebecca tilted back her own hat. "We'll try again tomorrow."

"Sure thing, boss." Ben uncapped his canteen. He took a long drink, the water dribbling over his chin and down his neck.

Rebecca opened her own canteen and let the water trickle down her throat. The tepid water tasted of metal, but it was still the sweetest thing she could remember drinking. Anyone who grew up in the desert, even that of the high plains, knew the dangers of dehydration.

A sigh escaped her lips when she recalled that some city-bred bureaucrat was due to arrive today to start tagging the existing wolves, hoping to bring in more.

Rebecca knew her men were waiting for her, but she motioned them on. She needed time alone. "I'll see you back at the ranch."

She watched as they rode off until they were no more than a puff of dust in the distance. Heat shimmered in waves, causing her to pull her hat further down to shade her eyes.

The hum of a plane overhead had her looking up. Someday, she vowed, she'd have one of her own, a small Cessna maybe. A rancher could save days, maybe weeks, with a plane to survey the land. All she needed now was the cash to buy one.

Yeah, right, she thought, like she had any extra cash. If she did, she'd hire a foreman to help manage the ranch. Then she'd be able to devote more time working with disabled children from the reservation, a project close to her heart.

Money was in short supply, and it didn't look like things were going to change anytime soon.

But it didn't hurt to dream.

Rebecca had learned early in life not to pin too much on dreams. Still, a few secret hopes that she'd hugged in the secret places of her heart persisted, undiminished by the realities of life.

Maggie neighed, an impatient reminder that she didn't like the inactivity.

Rebecca had raised the dainty mare from the time of her birth. Maggie was more than a faithful mount. She was a friend.

"Okay, girl," Rebecca murmured. She was in hour twelve of a day that showed no signs of ending anytime soon. She was ready to put her feet up and drink a gallon of lemonade, but she had some things to sort out. For that, she needed the peace she found only in the land.

She gave Maggie her attention. As if sensing Rebecca's mood, Maggie galloped over the ground with an easy stride that gave the illusion of flying. At last they pulled to a stop at a shelter of rocks.

There, away from everyone, she dismounted and

gazed over the prairie, frowning over the scant vegetation which was limited to the most hardy plants. Scrub brush, dried to the color of sage, dotted the ground. A lizard slithered across her boot. The sky was a kaleidoscope of color, gaudy against the dun-colored landscape.

The land pulled at Rebecca, as it always did. She hunkered down and picked up a handful of dirt. She lifted it to her nose and inhaled deeply before letting it sift through her fingers.

"You have the spirit of your ancestors running through your veins," Uncle Ray had told her long ago. "The kind of spirit that makes you fight when your land is threatened."

She hadn't understood what her uncle had meant at the time. Uncle Ray often talked in riddles, but Rebecca had taken the words to heart.

She loved the land, without reservation, without the uncertainty that colored almost every other aspect of her life. Her people had lived and died here; it was her birthright as well as her legacy.

Uncle Ray had made sure Rebecca respected the land as well as love it. She remembered a camping trip where Ray had taken her to one of the canyons that cut through the ranch. As they prepared to leave the following morning, Rebecca carelessly tossed the trash to the ground. Quietly, her uncle cleaned up the area, leaving it as pristine as when they came.

"Take nothing and leave nothing behind but your footprints."

Uncle Ray had never said another word to his niece about the incident. He hadn't needed to.

She stood, focusing her gaze on the range that stretched hundreds of miles in either direction. Scorched by the late summer heat, scarred by the wind that carved jagged ridges and deep valleys into it, the land was as harsh as it was beautiful. Too many had paid the ultimate price to protect what was theirs.

It was also hers. The land could be an exacting taskmaster. It demanded back-breaking work, sweat, blood, and every ounce of energy she had to give. And then some.

It had taken much of her youth and all of her adult life to build the ranch into something she could be proud of. It had demanded that she sacrifice everything she had just to hold onto it.

Out of habit, she scanned the sky, hoping the few clouds she saw there meant rain. A rancher spent a good part of his life praying for rain. Too little rain meant drought; too much, flooding.

She had learned to interpret nature's signs. A lifetime spent outdoors had taught her how to feel the changes coming. It was a good life. She couldn't imagine living anywhere else.

Love for the land, though, didn't blind her to the drawbacks of her home. Earth baked hard by the sun for five months needed a gentle rain. Too frequently, late summer storms pounded the ground ruthlessly. The shriveled earth had no chance to absorb the moisture, flooding the riverbeds and the surrounding plains.

Many a rancher had lost live stock due to flash floods. Many more lost stock to the effects of dehydration, and some, like her, lost animals to predators like Santanna.

Summer heat had sapped the land dry and the energy from all who made their living from it. Her own was fraying, along with her hope.

She squinted into the distance, absorbing the place she called home. The high desert was a study in contrasts, blistering hot during the day, cut-to-the-bone cold at night, but still she loved it.

The sky deepened in color as dusk approached. The sun slanted down below the peaks in the west, so the black shadow of the mountains inched lower on the canyon walls. The encroaching darkness mirrored her mood.

She flicked the reins. "Okay, Maggie. Home." The mare knew the way with scarcely a nudge from Rebecca.

So absorbed was she in her thoughts that she didn't register another rider's presence until he hailed her a second time. She reined Maggie to a stop and waited while the man and horse approached.

She approved the way he sat a horse, tall and straight in the saddle, alert to his surroundings but easy at the same time. The bay gelding he rode was every bit as compelling. She knew a moment's envy for the magnificent animal.

Her own horses ran more to working stock—sturdy, reliable. As though to atone for any disloyalty to her adored Maggie, Rebecca stroked the mare's neck.

Maggie responded to the gelding's presence with a toss of her head.

"Easy," Rebecca murmured, She flicked the reins over Maggie's neck with a whispered order to "Stay," then dismounted.

The other rider did the same.

She gave herself a moment to study him. His skin had a reddish tint beneath what she was sure was a newly-acquired tan. *A city fellow playing at being a cowboy*, she thought in disparagement. Then she recalled the familiar way he had with the big gelding. *Not such a city fellow after all*, she acknowledged grudgingly.

He didn't miss her quick inventory. She had the feeling that this man didn't miss much of anything.

She felt his swift assessment of her.

He stuck out his hand. "Matt McCall." His hand, large and hard, swallowed hers. "I'm from the Akela Foundation. The Foundation works to restore the balance of nature that man has destroyed. I'm here to—"

"I know why you're here," she said, and worked to ignore the needles of awareness that skittered up her arm at his touch.

She withdrew her hand and took a step back. She'd been expecting him. She'd heard that someone from the Akela Foundation was arriving to rebuild the wolf population in Colorado. She bit back a mirthless laugh.

Just what she and the other ranchers needed. More wolves.

After another minute, his name clicked into place. McCall. "Any relation to Amos McCall?"

One corner of his mouth lifted. "My grandfather."

She'd known Amos from years ago. He and Uncle Ray had been friends at a time when friendship between Native Americans and whites was still enough of a novelty to cause comment. "He was a good man."

"He was. He's part of the reason I'm here."

She understood family, understood the pull of blood. Wasn't that why she was fighting to hold onto the land she called home?

He closed the short distance between them which she'd created. Unlike many large men, Matt McCall wore his size comfortably, moving with an easy grace. Lanky, with longish hair and hawk-sharp eyes, he didn't look the part of the rumpled bureaucrat her imagination had conjured up.

She held her ground, tilting her head in order to meet his gaze. She wasn't accustomed to that and didn't care for it. At five feet ten inches, she was as tall as most men, taller than many. Her chin came up in automatic reaction.

There was a stillness about him, the patient stillness of a predator as it stalks its quarry, and all at once, she was reminded of Santanna.

Her skin prickled with tension as the man made no pretense of not staring at her. Attraction arced between them, an intangible but nonetheless real force. A rush of air signaled that she'd been holding her breath. She inhaled sharply, hoping the influx of oxygen would clear her head.

It didn't.

Tension rippled in waves so intense that she was surprised the air didn't snap with electricity. She lowered her gaze, and the spell was broken.

She let her gaze slide down the length of him. There wasn't an ounce of extra flesh on him, she noted, nor an ounce of softness. The firm set of his mouth, the strong line of his shoulders, the startling blue gaze that held both integrity and strength, all bore the stamp of a man who knew what he was about.

Like Santanna, he wouldn't be an easy enemy to defeat.

The brief conversation had given Matt time to study Rebecca and form some conclusions of his own.

Some Native American blood, he decided, would account for the slash of cheekbones and high brow. Hair the color of a sleek raven was caught at her neck by a leather thong. Her skin was as gold as the sun, her eyes a darker shade of the same.

She fit here. Not just in the way she was dressed—the leather vest worn over a denim shirt and well-worn jeans. It was in the way she held herself, the way she was at one with the land. Confidence gave her an air of command.

"I heard they were sending some kind of expert with a string of fancy letters after his name."

He waited as she gave him another thorough scrutiny.

"Whatever I expected, it sure wasn't you."

"Let me guess. You expected a little man in glasses with his head bent over a clipboard and a calculator in his pocket."

This time the smile went all the way to her eyes. It changed her face, made it radiant.

"How'd you know?" she asked.

"Just naturally smart," he said around a smile that matched hers.

She rocked back on her heels, thumbs hooked in her pockets. "People around here don't have much use for thieves, especially the four-legged variety."

"Thieves?"

"That's right. A pack of wolves has been making off with sheep from the ranchers. My flock was hit a couple of nights ago."

Twin grooves formed between his brows. "You're running your sheep on an open range?"

"Look around you. We're in the middle of a drought. I have to use every bit of range I have just to keep my stock alive."

He followed her gaze and saw what she meant. The sun-scorched ground with its almost non-existent vegetation was mute evidence of the drought. "How long?"

She swiped at her face with a sweat-stained bandanna. "Three years."

"It looks bad."

She slanted him a faintly derisive glance. "What's the matter? Don't you like the effects of a drought?"

The temper in her voice was more than a match for the heat that blanketed the land.

He ignored it. "Your sheep—are you sure it was wolves that killed them?"

"I'm sure."

"You've got a chip on your shoulder, Ms. White-feather."

"Make it Rebecca. And it's no chip. What I've got are too many bills and a pack of wolves bent on destroying my livelihood."

He didn't blame her. How could he? But it didn't change what he had to do.

"Santanna and his marauders took three of my best sheep," she said. "One had a belly full of lambs."

"Santanna?"

She flushed. "The leader. A big black. I named him that the first time he showed up."

He heard the thread of emotion in her voice, saw the change in her eyes. "You like him."

She dipped her head. The movement made light shimmer on her dark hair. "I did."

"Did, as in past tense?"

"You got it."

"I'm sorry for your troubles, but nothing you've said changes what I have to do." He'd known he'd face opposition for the job he came here to do, but he hadn't counted on encountering it so soon.

"I didn't think it would." She gave him another measuring look. "You're in for a fight."

He grinned. "Have you always been like this?"

"Like what?"

"Hard-headed."

"Yeah." Determination radiated from her. "I respect what you're trying to do, but you don't understand what you're up against."

The impatience had left her voice. It was quiet now, and controlled, but something else lay just beneath. He tried to pinpoint what it was. Desperation. Fear.

She wouldn't admit to it, he realized. A woman like Rebecca Whitefeather wouldn't like acknowledging anything akin to weakness. Though he had just met her, he felt her strength. She was as proud and unyielding as the land where she made her home.

At the same time, he felt the air of vulnerability that pulsated off her in tense waves. He studied her profile, taking in the weariness that shadowed her eyes and pulled at the corners of her mouth.

Her gaze was focused on a horizon only she could see. He didn't believe she was ignoring him, but was immersing herself in the land.

He'd grown away from the land he'd loved as a child, but he remembered what his grandfather had felt for it, the reverence with which he'd treated it.

He was beginning to understand Rebecca's attitude toward the wolves. It didn't change what he had to do, but he softened his tone and put out a hand to touch her arm. At the contact, he felt the energy arc through the air, forming a bridge between them. "Listen, Ms. Whitefeather—"

"It's Rebecca," she reminded him.

"Okay. Rebecca. I understand how you feel, but—"

"You have no idea how I feel. How could you? You're barely here an hour and you think you know how I feel?" The impatience was back. In spades.

Too late, he recognized how arrogant his words must have sounded. He was a newcomer here. He knew enough to realize it would take time to gain acceptance.

"Sorry. I didn't mean to offend you." He took a deep breath and decided he'd better get it over with. "But I'm here to do a job. I'm not leaving until it's done."

She leveled a long gaze at him. "You have a job to do. And so do I." She tossed her head as though issuing a challenge, and wispy tendrils of hair danced around her face.

"You don't back down easy, do you?" he asked.

"No."

He liked her straight-forward manner of speaking with no pretty words attached. At the same time, he noticed one more thing about her: She had a stubborn line to her mouth. "You're not what I expected," he said, using her own words.

"Same here."

Chapter Two

At thirty-four years old, Matt McCall had declared his independence.

He'd taken the degree in natural sciences he'd earned a dozen years ago, before he'd been sucked into his father's corporation, and applied for a job with the Akela Foundation, a non-profit organization devoted to restoring wild animals to their natural habitat. His first assignment, transporting gray wolves to their former home in the Southwest, had brought him here, to Miracle, Colorado.

It seemed fitting, he thought, that he was returning the wolves to the one place he had ever called home.

Whatever became of his "fool notion," as his father called it, Matt didn't regret his decision to leave the corporate world. Nor did he regret leaving the controlling influence of Erskin McCall. He'd resigned from his father's oil company where he'd held the position of vice-president.

For too long, Matt had towed the line, had been the dutiful son who didn't question what was expected of him, until his father had betrayed them both. Erskin had skirted the law in the past, but this time, he'd gone too far with his flouting of the standards laid down by the EPA. For Matt, for anyone who believed as passionately in protecting the environment as he did, that had crossed the line.

Erskin McCall was a self-avowed workaholic who had had little time for his wife, son, or anyone else. Matt had long ago accepted that his father wouldn't be there for Little League or high school baseball games. He'd even missed the championship game in Matt's senior year.

Matt didn't have any illusions about his place in the scheme of his father's life. What he couldn't accept was the old man's lack of ethics. His determination to go with a disreputable dumping company had triggered Matt's decision to leave, though it had been brewing within him for a long while.

The falling out with his father had hurt, but it couldn't be helped. Father and son had both said things they'd regretted, but pride and a large dose of ego on both sides had kept them from making it up.

Matt put the past from his mind. He was here to start a new life.

The desert in early morning was deceiving, cool despite the heat the rapidly rising sun promised. He'd opted for a T-shirt and comfortable jeans. With sunglasses and a ball cap to protect his face, he was dressed for a day in the Colorado desert. He had a notepad stuffed in his pocket and his mind working overtime.

He didn't push the gelding on the return to his grandfather's cabin. He wanted to take his time, to feel the land.

He was here to start a new life, in more ways than one.

Matt had known he wouldn't be welcomed in Miracle. His chance meeting with Rebecca Whitefeather yesterday only confirmed what he'd already known.

He hadn't been back to the small town since his grandfather had died over ten years ago. He let out the breath he hadn't realized he was holding and looked around.

The land never failed to arouse a strong feeling of connection within him. He'd felt it years ago when he'd come here as a child. The feeling had lain dormant for years, but now it tugged at him, reminding him that, for a few summers, this had been home.

He had forgotten the stunning beauty of the high plains of southern Colorado. Nothing had prepared him for the sight of the purple-banded prairie and a sky so big that it seemed to go on forever. Towering mountains ringed the wide valley, their summits sporting snug caps of snow.

He stared at the expanse of land, knowing that over

five hundred acres were his. Not much in comparison to the other land-owners, but they belonged to him.

His property. He'd never thought of himself as a landowner, but he realized he liked the idea, especially since that land had once belonged to his grandfather. When he'd taken sick, the land had been sold for back taxes.

Since then it had traded hands several times. It had taken every bit of Matt's savings to scrape together enough to buy it.

It had been worth it.

That brought him full circle to the thing that had brought him here. The wolves. He had a job to do, and he didn't intend on letting anything—or anyone—interfere with that, even a woman as appealing as Rebecca Whitefeather.

For the first time in his life, he was doing something for himself.

Independence felt good, he decided. He could practically taste it. To his mind, it had the same tang as the mountain-fresh air of the his new home.

Matt had grown up on stories of the Old West. Ever since he could remember, his grandfather had regaled him with tales of round-ups, cattle drives, and rodeos. He'd outlived the days when cowboys and their horses were the backbone of the sprawling cattle ranches to be replaced by pickup trucks and helicopters.

But he'd instilled in Matt the excitement, the

romance, and the energy of the era. The young Matt had taken his grandfather's words to heart.

The seeds Amos had planted had taken root, and Matt had known from an early age that he'd return to this land someday and make it his home. The journey had taken longer than he'd planned, but he was here now.

He remembered the sadness in his grandfather's voice when he'd told Matt about the bounties put on gray wolves to rid the state of them. The ranchers had banded together and set out to exterminate the animals.

Amos's eyes had filled with tears as he'd recalled how bounty hunters had set steel traps that broke the animals' legs and left them to starve to death. The proud animals which had once roamed from Mexico to Alaska in packs numbering in the thousands were now reduced to a pitiful few.

"I was part of it," Amos said. "It shames me to own up to it, that I had anything to do with destroying the wolves. I'd give everything I have if I could undo what I did."

The words were as clear today as they had been two decades ago. That had been the only time Matt had ever seen his grandfather give way to tears.

Coming to Colorado, helping to restore the wolves to their former home, was for his granddad, and, he admitted, for himself. He couldn't stop his father from defiling the land, but he could make a difference here, and, in a small way, atone for the sins his family had committed.

If Matt could complete this project of bringing in wolves from Canada to strengthen the existing packs, it would go a long way to righting the wrongs that had been committed over a half century ago. Only a few dozen wolves existed in the state, and those that did were regarded as nuisances by the ranchers.

He refused to consider the possibility that he might not succeed.

He'd studied maps of the area and zeroed in on a likely spot for the pack to make their den. He settled his hat more firmly on his head, nudged Trapper with his heels, and started off.

An hour later, he was watching for any sign of the wolves. Never one of his virtues, his patience was being stretched to the limit as he waited.

Shading his eyes from the glare of the sun, he peered into the distance and spotted a cloud of dust. Could he possibly be lucky enough to catch a glimpse of the wolves on his second day here? Telling himself not to expect too much, he headed in that direction.

He wasn't sure how far he'd gone, but the cloud had disappeared.

He looked around, trying to get his bearings. In the heat of late August, the land was hard and unyielding. Desert-yellow, it could be cruel, extracting a price from those not experienced in its ways, but it was also magnificent. Its stark beauty pulled at him just as it had that first time so many summers ago.

Matt patted Trapper's neck. He'd bought the animal

on impulse from a local rancher. He hadn't regretted the purchase. Already horse and man had established a bond.

He let Trapper have his head, reveling in the horse's power as his legs ate up the miles with effortless speed. The animal understood what Matt needed before he did himself.

The land was like the wolves he was trying so hard to save, wild, free, and unclaimed. A dry wind whipped across his face, stinging his eyes with sand. He brushed it away and then licked his lips.

The sun beat down upon him. His clothes were covered with brown dust by the time he reached the cabin, his throat drier than the bottom of an empty well.

He caught a gamey whiff of his own sweat and grinned. When was the last time he'd actually worked up a sweat? Too long, he thought.

His thoughts drifted to Rebecca Whitefeather. He'd bet that the pretty Native American didn't turn up her nose at hard work and honest sweat.

The lady was an enigma. Cool and aloof one moment, warm and friendly the following, angry and disapproving the next. He had a feeling he could like her under different circumstances. He shook his head and sighed in regret. Fate had put them on opposite sides of the fence.

Her obvious love for the land was something he could understand and respect. Hadn't his grandfather felt the same way? He'd believed the land was a trust, passed down from one generation to the next.

No one could own it, Amos had told Matt more than once. He'd passed on his love for the land as well as the wolves to his grandson.

Matt had made a trip to town where he'd purchased a store of supplies, letting it be known that he was here to stay.

The townspeople had reacted with curiosity to downright hostility. Neither had come as a surprise. He approached the project with the same thoroughness as he would a business deal. Gather information, analyze it, make informed decisions.

He followed the clamor of yelps and howls to find a scraggly patch of scrub oak and fir. There, a pack of wolves frolicked in the sun.

He let out a low whistle as he watched the leader of the pack, a big black who stood out among the motley assortment of gray and rust-colored animals. He must weigh at least a hundred and thirty pounds. The alpha male.

Could he be Santanna?

The animal fit the description Rebecca had given. Matt now understood the note of respect he'd heard in her voice. How could anyone not admire such a magnificent animal? How could anyone want to destroy him?

Watching Santanna, he understood that the animal belonged to the land as surely as did the prairie grass and the sand lizards.

A half-dozen other wolves bore a striking resemblance to him. Probably his off-spring, Matt decided. Most of the rest were a straggly-looking bunch of crossbreeds. With blood from various breeds, including coyotes, the wolves had become a mongrel mix.

Bringing in a dozen gray wolves from Canada would go a long way in restoring the bloodline. What wolves that had survived the extermination of decades ago had migrated to Canada. The biologists at the Akela Foundation believed that, with the proper nurturing, the gray wolves would not only survive but thrive in their new surroundings.

First, though, he needed to study the few wolves remaining here, learn their habits, understand how the introduction of new animals would affect the existing pack.

Wolves were social creatures, their community a clearly defined pecking order.

He noted a dozen or so pups in the pack, a few more yearlings. He spent another fifteen minutes watching them and admiring the leader.

The sun beat down with merciless intensity. Matt pushed his hat back and let the slight breeze cool his forehead. Taking the kerchief from around his neck, he wiped the perspiration from his face and thought ruefully of the full canteen he'd left sitting on the kitchen table.

Only a tenderfoot went off without a canteen.

The nickname brought a smile to his lips. His grandfather had called Matt that the first summer he'd spent in Colorado. It had been a source of pride that Amos hadn't had cause to apply it to Matt again. From the time he was ten until he'd started college, he'd spent every summer here.

His smile faded as he realized how far away from the land he'd grown in the intervening years. He'd rationalized his long absence by reminding himself he'd been busy with getting his education and starting a job, but he knew it was more than that. He hadn't been able to face the memories.

The land was so tied to his grandfather that he couldn't think of one without remembering the other. He shook away the sadness and reminded himself of his promise to remember the good times.

Amos had believed in living to the fullest. Even when cancer had riddled his body with pain, he'd kept his sense of humor and tart tongue.

Matt watched as the pups romped and cavorted in the sun like frisky puppies. They butted each other with their heads, pranced off, and returned to start the game all over again.

A pale gray wolf, probably the alpha female, bossed her way through the pack and howled, a signal for the pups to follow. When a few remained, she nipped at them until they obeyed. She deposited a ground squirrel in the center of a clearing.

One pup, nearly black, was the first to approach. He anticipated the prey's movements and countered by blocking and feinting. More than once, he was bitten and bleeding before he learned to dodge and lunge at the right time.

The others took their turns. When one was injured, he limped back to the female, who consoled him and tenderly licked his wounds. Their play had a purpose. In a few months they would learn to tackle larger prey.

It was like a small community, Matt thought, complete with leaders and followers, rewards and penalties.

His attention focused once more on Santanna. He was one of the most beautiful animals Matt had ever seen. He was also cautious, Matt noted, as he saw the ears flick forward. What had he heard?

Matt listened intently but couldn't hear anything except for the rustling of the wind.

Santanna gave a howl to his pack.

Another wolf, a rare blue-gray, emerged. One of the yearlings, he paced around Santanna, his tail held high in challenge.

He watched as the two wolves stalked and nipped at each other. Santanna lunged low, attacking and finding the vulnerable neck of the upstart. The blue-gray skulked off, tail down now, clearly beaten.

Matt hadn't realized he was holding his breath until now. He expelled it in a low whistle. It was a hierarchy, not so different from that in the corporate world from which he'd so recently escaped.

He heard the approach of a rider. A different kind of awareness flickered through him. He didn't need his eyes to tell him what his other senses already had. Rebecca Whitefeather had worked her way into his mind last night and had refused to budge.

She dismounted and tethered Maggie. "Magnificent, aren't they?" she asked when she came to stand at his side.

She was tall, comfortable against his own six feet two, and slender, but beneath the willowy build, he sensed strength. Her hands were ringless and practical, the unpolished nails cut short and square.

"I've never seen anything so wild. Or so beautiful," he said, his voice husky with feeling, but his gaze was on her.

"One goes with the other."

He tipped back his hat. He heard the half-sad, half-admiring note in her voice and stared at her, surprised at the depth of feeling he read in her face. She'd been as moved by the display as he had.

Her inky black hair and golden eyes set in a strong face were unforgettable, but it was the thrust of her chin that was the most telling. The lady was no quitter.

She was a woman who drew a man's gaze, not because she was beautiful, although she was far from plain, but because she compelled attention.

The morning sun glinted off her hair, untidy, as though she'd run her fingers through it. Dimples dented her cheeks, and her eyes were slanted against the glare of the sun. *No man alive*, he thought, *could resist the picture she made.*

It was a face that radiated too much strength to be merely pretty. Dark gold eyes squarely met his gaze.

He couldn't have said how long they spent there, content to simply watch the animals.

"They're like children," he said. "Wrestling with each other, each trying to best the next. Don't you see that they have to be preserved?"

She shrugged off his hand. "Things change. Times change. People change." Regret, sharp and sweet, tinged her voice.

"You care about the wolves. I hear it in your voice and see it in your eyes, whenever you talk about them.

"How could you want to destroy something like Santanna? He belongs here." He gestured to encompass the vast plain. Even now, with the land scorched by the unrelenting sun, the prairie with its flanking of mountains was beautiful.

"I agree."

"Then you won't try to kill him?"

"I didn't say that."

"It all comes down to the bottom line, doesn't it?" he asked, reminded of his father and his obsession to acquire more and more money, along with more and more power.

"You better believe it. Ranching isn't some game we're playing at. It's what we do . . . who we are." He saw the conflict in her eyes and knew that she was trying to convince herself as well as him.

He studied the woman who seemed determined to

challenge him on every level. At the same time, he felt the energy arc through the air, forming a bridge between them.

Tension bunched along her shoulders. The strain he'd noticed in her upon their first meeting had deepened. He recognized the signs. Until a month ago, he'd worn the same marks of stress.

Looking into her clear eyes, he knew she wouldn't back down. He'd expected no less.

The anger slid out of him as he realized she was doing the same thing that he was: fighting for what she believed.

He needed time, to understand the effect she had on him, to figure out why she had managed to get under his skin in a way no other woman had.

Sure, he was attracted to her. What man wouldn't respond to a woman as intelligent, sharp, and vital as Rebecca? But he was drawn to her in a way that defied the reason and sense that he brought to every other aspect of his life.

With a curt good-bye, she headed back to the little mare she'd been riding the first time he'd seen her.

He watched her sleek gait. He liked the way she moved, her long legs striking out as though she had places to go, things to do. Before he had a chance to talk himself out of it, he followed her.

She turned. "Did you want something?" There was something about the thrust of her chin, the way that she held herself, that made him think she was preparing for battle.

"I thought you might show me around." For a minute, he thought she might refuse, then her smile unfurled.

"All right."

She set a leisurely pace, and he felt her relax degree by degree. Her smile came more readily as she talked about the town and its people, and he added one more piece to the puzzle of Rebecca Whitefeather: she was fiercely loyal to her friends.

Her smile curled up and died when they spotted two vultures circling low in the sky. By silent agreement, they headed in that direction.

The air grew thick, the smell unmistakable. Blood. Just like that, the easy camaraderie between them had vanished, and in its place was a tension so taut it was nearly palpable.

They found what was left of the ewe on the southern border of her property.

Before he could help her, she'd dismounted and walked to where the carcass had already started to attract flies. She knelt beside it, her eyes shimmering with unshed tears. "This is my fault. I refused to set traps." Her voice had a bitter, rusty edge that they both felt.

He silently applauded her refusal to use the cruel traps, even while he witnessed the pain in her eyes, shiny with unshed tears. It wasn't only the financial loss of the animal, though he knew that her operation ran close to the bone. She ached for the death of the creature.

He wanted to reach for her, to pull her to him and

offer what comfort he could. He might have done just that, but she walked back to Maggie.

She opened her saddlebags, and withdrew a small, folded shovel. "It comes in handy," she said.

Without being told, he knew that this wasn't the first time she'd had to perform this grisly act.

He looked at her. Her eyes were no longer on the verge of overflowing; they were hard now. Her hands were steady on the shovel.

He made to reach for it.

She spun away. "My sheep, my responsibility."

He started to object, but saw the grim purpose in her gaze, and shut up.

It took every ounce of self-control he possessed not to take the shovel from her as she pushed it into the sun-baked ground, over and over, digging a grave.

Finally when the hole was large enough, he lifted the animal, put it in the ground, and refilled the hole.

When he finished, he turned to her, needing to say something, but knowing that whatever he said, it could never be enough.

He didn't think she was aware of it, but she had wrapped her arms around her middle, as if trying to block out the scene. The defensive stance made her appear younger and infinitely vulnerable.

"What did you expect?" she asked when the silence between them had stretched to the breaking point.

He winced. He understood her anger, but was surprised by the responding chord he felt within himself.

He had no answers for her, no *easy* answers at any rate. The wolves had killed one of her flock. How had he ever expected her to accept him or his job?

He'd come here to reintroduce wolves to what had once been their home, but he was beginning to understand that there was much more involved than he had realized. If he were to do his job, he needed to help find an answer for the wolves *and* the ranchers.

For all his belief in his job and the rightness of what he was doing, it was difficult to contemplate the savagery of the wolves and maintain his objectivity. So far, few things in Miracle were as he'd anticipated.

That included Rebecca. Her gaze was far away now, where distant pines turned the mountain black.

Though he wasn't touching her, he could almost feel her spine stiffen, the delicate vertebrae snap into place. Her eyes were shuttered against giving anything more away. He'd learned to recognize that look even in the short time he'd known her, the one that told him to back off.

Frustration washed over him, even though he understood her anger and sympathized with it.

"I'm sorry." He winced at the emptiness of the apology.

The words hung between them, a barrier which neither could breach. Battle lines had been drawn.

Chapter Three

Rebecca did her best to put Matt McCall out of her mind for the days that followed. The demands of the ranch helped in that regard. So did her decision to attend an emergency town meeting with the other ranchers.

"I hear you're spending time with that city fellow who wants to sic the wolves on us," Rudy Novak said as she took a seat near the front of the community center.

"I'm showing him both sides of the story," Rebecca returned in an even voice.

Rudy had been a braggart and a bully in high school. He hadn't changed in the ten years since graduation. He'd been one of the first to suggest hunting down the wolves.

Though his idea had been voted down, it didn't stop him from stirring up trouble whenever he could get anyone to listen. Like now.

"Why don't you tell us more about this man?" Joe Running Deer, the reservation representative, asked Rebecca.

Rebecca chose her words with care. The time she'd spent with Matt had stirred her own protective feelings toward the wolves. "He's intelligent. What's more, he genuinely cares about the environment."

"One of those tree huggers," Novak said with a sneer.

She ignored that. "If we hope to protect our stock, we have to find a way to work with him."

She came away from the meeting more frustrated and confused than ever. She couldn't fault the others for wanting to put an end to the wolves' raiding their cattle and sheep.

Inexorably, her thoughts were pulled back to the afternoon when she and Matt had found the sheep. Honesty forced her to admit that his job hadn't caused the destruction of the animal. No matter how hard she tried, though, she couldn't separate what he was trying to do from the loss of the ewe.

She thought of the man from the Akela Foundation. No, he hadn't been what she'd expected. The man was entirely too sure of himself, entirely too attractive, entirely too everything for a woman's peace of mind.

A frown pleated her forehead. Just when and how

had she allowed herself to become so darned aware of him as a man? She'd met him less than a week ago. So why did she find herself thinking about him at odd hours? Just because he had blue eyes that could melt a woman's bones at one hundred paces?

Because she had no answer to that—no acceptable answer anyway—she pushed it from her mind. Matt McCall wasn't something she was prepared to deal with. Not yet.

She'd heard that he had purchased supplies in town, a sign that he was planning to stay.

Memories of the way his gaze had connected with hers, the warmth of his fingers as they'd closed around her own, skittered over her.

It would have been better, she thought, *if he'd been the bureaucrat of her imagination with a pocket protector, soft, pampered hands, a calculator in one hand, and a ledger in the other*. She recognized the conjured-up picture as ridiculous. Still, it had been a comforting one.

She recalled his help when they'd stumbled upon the sheep carcass. He'd wanted to take the chore of burying the animal from her.

She returned to the ranch but didn't go inside immediately. It was one of those evenings when twilight refused to hurry. Heat still hung heavily over the land, but a breeze feathered over her face, bringing a moment's relief.

Sleep eluded her that night, as she tussled over the problem of the wolves.

She headed to the barn just as dawn made its appearance. A ride would smooth away the rough edges of a rough night. The soft whickerings and pungent smell of horses soothed her as nothing else could.

"Hey there, beautiful lady. Are you feeling frisky this morning?" Rebecca asked, sidestepping as Maggie tried to nip her. "Up for a ride?"

A whicker answered in the affirmative.

Clouds scuttled across the morning gray, the sun but a kiss on the horizon.

Rebecca took the path from the valley up to the foothills at an easy pace. In the distance, snow topped the mountains, dribbling down them like whipped cream atop a hot-fudge sundae.

Even at early morning, the day was as bright as a child's paintbox of colors, the sky so blue it hurt the eyes to stare into it, the landscape done up fancy with vivid pinks and purples under the gleam of the sun. It was the desert at its best.

A plaintive cry echoed over the prairie.

The wolf's howl was eerily melancholy and heart-breakingly wistful. Hunger throbbed in it—hunger for its mate, for offspring, for life.

It was close. Too close.

Stay in the mountains, she prayed. *If you come down, you'll be killed.*

The animal howled again.

She shivered, more in response to the wolf's bay than to the early morning chill.

Her thoughts strayed to Matt.

He was someone she could like, perhaps more than like, but she feared their loyalties would always divide them. Her thoughts churned inside her mind.

She wanted to know him better. He intrigued her. A self-admitted refugee from the corporate world, he didn't seem the type to be tackling this kind of assignment.

He'd been a surprise, in more ways than one. He had callouses, she remembered. Hard ridges across his palms that no pencil pusher should have known how to acquire. The thought gave her pause. No, he wasn't what he expected, not in the least.

The screech of a hawk had her looking up. The sight of the bird gliding through the sky transfixed her. She watched as it swooped to pounce upon a ground squirrel, then soar upward once more, the prey caught in its powerful talons.

Some might be repelled by the scene. She knew better, understanding it was but one part of nature's cycle. Each part had its place, a piece of the whole.

City folk didn't understand. Unbidden, a picture of Matt formed in her mind. Would he, she wondered. Would he understand that nature wasn't always tidy? That it couldn't always be wrapped up in facts and figures and made to fit some preconceived idea?

She was surprised—and dismayed—to find that the answer mattered.

She breathed with the sounds of the desert. The chirping of crickets, the croak of a toad, each as famil-

iar as her own heartbeat, filled the night. The slither of
a lizard, the scuttling of a small animal, and the constant hum of the wind generated a harmony that rivaled
that of renowned symphonies.

She remembered the noises that routinely bombard-
ed her ears in the city. Horns blasting, sirens screaming,
and engines roaring were a poor substitute for the
music that serenaded her now.

How could anyone prefer the suffocation of the city,
she wondered, where a person felt smothered with too
many people, too many things.

She recalled a recent trip to Denver. The streets were
choked with cars and indignant drivers, the buildings a
gaudy parody of skyscraping mountains, the houses
bunched close together with scarcely a slice of sky
between them. Tourists, attracted by the boom of the
arts and crafts movement, had invaded the city with
their expensive cars, expensive tastes, and expensive
demands.

She could hardly take a step without bumping into
someone. It was a pretty enough city, she supposed, if
you liked all the noise and confusion. The sheer num-
ber of people, where everyone seemed in a desperate
rush to get somewhere other than where they were, had
made her yearn for the quiet, lazy pace of home and the
clean air that was perfumed by the scent of sun and
earth rather than that of exhaust.

Of course, a city-dweller might see things different-
ly, might not feel the tug of the land, the freedom of the

open range, the vastness of the desert that stretched endlessly in all directions.

Matt had a job to do. So did she. Her job was to save her ranch. She knew her motives weren't altruistic. It was a matter of survival.

An idea took root in her mind. If she could make Matt understand what the loss of the sheep meant, he might give up his plan to introduce more wolves to the region.

If she could convince Matt that the livelihood of nearly everyone in the area depended upon keeping their stock safe, maybe he'd abandon the plan of bringing more wolves here.

She'd lay on the charm. After all, sugar caught more flies than vinegar. She'd introduce him to the other ranchers, let him see what they were up against.

Rebecca didn't like what she was planning, but she didn't have a choice. She had to convince Matt that the wolves were destroying what it had taken several life-times to build.

Santanna and his pack were robbing her and the other ranchers blind.

Given the uncertain price of wool, the losses due to the drought, and the constant outlay for new equipment, the margin profit in sheep ranching was minimal even in good years. Add to that the loss of a dozen of her sheep, and she was looking at some hard times.

Ever since she'd been big enough to ride a horse, she'd worked to build the ranch back to what it had been before her parents had died. It'd taken every bit of energy and every cent she had ... plus some she hadn't. She'd paid off the last of the bank note only last year. For the first time in almost twenty years, the ranch was free and clear.

Dust swelled in the distance, signalling the approach of a rider. She tilted her hat back and recognized Matt.

Once again, he sat astride the bay gelding. He dismounted and walked in her direction.

She did the same.

They took each other's measure.

After a minute's study, she had to look away from the tall, lean strength of him and was chagrined to realize that she was fighting a hopeless attraction to a man she had no reason to like. His very presence clogged her brain until she could scarcely form a coherent thought.

She hardened her resolve for what she was about to do. "I think we got off on the wrong foot. My fault. I'd like to make it up to you. Maybe show you around."

He looked surprised, then pleased. "I'd like that."

She showed him the secluded meadow where she kept the lambs and ewes. She dismounted and went straight for them, cuddling them to her, heedless of the dirt and burrs that clung to their fleece.

Matt followed at a slower pace.

Her breath caught in her throat at what she saw in his eyes, as if he'd come upon something precious and rare. He cared. She saw it in his compassion-warmed eyes. The thought gave her hope.

Her sheep dog, a feisty terrier, gave a sharp yelp. The sheep lifted their heads, nudged their lambs to their feet, and prepared to follow.

She dusted off her jeans and started back to her mount. She showed him the scent posts made by Santanna and the other marauding wolves.

"It's even more beautiful than I remembered," he said.

Pride and hope welled within her. It underscored her words. "You understand."

"I understand you love this place. So do I."

They returned to his cabin in silence. A comfortable, friendly silence, suited to two people who were in accord with each other and their surroundings.

They spent the next days together.

When Rebecca suggested that she introduce him to some of the other ranchers, he accepted eagerly.

"You set an early pace," he said when they met early one morning. The sun had scarcely cleared the horizon.

"Morning is the best time in the desert."

He silently agreed. The temperature had already started to climb.

"Don't expect a welcoming committee," she warned. "Rudy Novak volunteered his place for us to meet the other ranchers, but don't let that fool you. Rudy's bone mean, but he wields a lot of influence in the area."

Matt had a feeling that Rebecca wielded some influence herself, though of a quieter nature. It was more important than ever that she understand what was at stake. If she could accept that, then maybe . . . He gave her a long look and saw the concern in her eyes. She *did* understand.

They covered the distance to Novak's place, talking little.

Rebecca introduced him to the half-dozen men and then stepped back.

He talked and, more importantly, listened, learning more about the effects of the drought, the financial problems that everyone in the valley faced.

"I come from the corporate world," he said. "I know how important the bottom line is. I'm working to find a way to relocate the wolves and to protect your stock."

"Very smooth," Rudy said with an ill-concealed sneer. "How you planning on going about it?"

"I don't know," Matt admitted. "Yet."

"At least that's honest," one of the men said and stuck out his hand. "Jacob Three Eagles."

Matt took the other man's hand, found it ridged with callus and scarred from a lifetime of working with animals.

"Most of us," Jacob said with a meaningful look in Rudy's direction, "don't want to see the wolves destroyed. But we have people who depend on us, if we lose our stock, everybody in the valley loses."

Matt digested that and listened as the other men expressed similar feelings. He was beginning to understand that the job he'd undertaken had many more sides than he'd first believed.

Several minutes later, Rebecca signalled that it was time to be on their way.

"Thanks for showing me around," he said as they headed back to his cabin.

"I didn't do it for you."

"I know. I also know you don't want to see Santanna and his pack destroyed. Why is it so hard for you to admit that?"

"I've never wanted that. But I'm a realist. I have to be. I know how you feel about the wolves. All city folk think there's something romantic about them."

"I'm not city folk—"

She ignored his protest. "Comes from watching too many Westerns on TV and at the movies. What you don't realize is the damage they do to all of us. It's not just the ranchers who don't like them. They go after the farmers' livestock and raid their hen houses."

"So the farmers don't like them either, huh?"

"No one who makes his living from the land likes them." She speared him with a hard look and pointed to the horizon, a strip of purple that banded the prairie. "See that?"

He let his gaze follow where she pointed, trying to understand what she was talking about.

"The land," she said, impatience simmering in her voice. "The land. It's what this is all about. The land is a living thing. It's what makes us what we are."

"We?"

"The people who make their living from it. And that

means just about everyone around here. The land's a part of us. When something threatens it, we fight back. We have to. We don't have a choice."

Neither did he. "Returning the wolves to where they belong is right."

"You call setting a bunch of wolves free to kill sheep and cattle right? You call destroying how we make our living right?" She gave him a derisive look. "You've got a funny way of looking at things."

"You're painting the worst case scenario," he said.

"I'm not painting anything," she tossed the words back at him. "I'm telling you what's happened in the past and what will happen again." She met his gaze unflinchingly.

She was facing him down, he thought with reluctant admiration, in a way no one has since he'd been a green kid and joined his father's business.

The lady was tough. He respected that. He allowed himself a more thorough study of her. He'd been right the first time. She was striking, even more so now with her eyes shooting sparks at him and her cheeks bright with color.

He reached for her hand. "I didn't take this job to win a popularity contest."

She looked at him thoughtfully. "No. I don't suppose you did."

"The wolves should be here in two days." He quietly added.

"You're still going through with it?" Rebecca asked.

"Did you think that I wouldn't?"

"You probably won't believe this," she said at last, "but I'm thinking about you as well as the ranchers."

He waited for her to continue.

"If you do what you're intending, you're going to destroy any chance you ever had of making a life here. Folks here have long memories. They're reserving judgment about you so far because of your grandfather, but—"

"I didn't come here to cause trouble, but I don't expect you to believe that."

At some point, their hands had fallen apart. A symbol, he wondered, of the differences that divided them?

"Looks like we've got an old-fashioned standoff," he said.

"Looks like."

"Maybe I can change your mind."

"Maybe you can't."

Was that regret he saw in her eyes? "I have to do this. I don't have a choice." He was talking about more than his job, much more. "You have a job to do. So do I. Did you think you could talk me out of it?"

The stricken expression on her face made him realize that that was exactly what she'd been attempting. Introducing him to the ranchers, talking of the plight of all those who were affected by the drought as well as the wolves, showing him around the community and making him feel a part of it, had all been part of convincing him to leave his job.

"I get it," he said slowly. "You thought if you showed me around, showed me what the land meant to you and the other ranchers, I'd change my mind. Tell the Foundation it won't work."

Disappointment sluiced through him, and with it, a renewed determination. He tightened his hands around the reins and gazed into the distance, absorbing the beauty of the rugged prairie.

A harsh land that turned its inhabitants equally harsh, he wondered. He rejected the notion as soon as it formed. Rebecca wasn't like that. He couldn't have been mistaken about her feelings for the wolves.

She was as much a part of the land as were the animals that made their home here. They both belonged. He'd make her see it, make her understand that she couldn't destroy the wolves without destroying a part of herself.

He took a minute to study her and frowned at the purple shadows under her eyes. Another sleepless night, he presumed, coupled with unanswered questions and too many worries piled upon her slender shoulders.

"Is it wrong to want to defend what's mine?" she asked, her voice as gritty as a desert sandstorm.

Her question dragged him back to reality with a jolt. He wouldn't get anywhere now, he realized. Some of the day's brightness dimmed, though the sun continued to beat down upon them.

His grandfather had lived and died here; it was his

heritage as much as Rebecca's, and he intended to preserve it, even if he had to fight her and all the other ranchers to do it.

The last thing, the very last thing, he could do was to lose sight of his mission. He'd made a promise to his grandfather, and to himself, and no one, not even the beautiful Rebecca Whitefeather, was going to keep him from fulfilling it.

Chapter Four

Three days later, Rebecca still felt the sting of Matt's disappointment in her for trying to talk him out of his job.

She put her back into cleaning out the barn. Sweat and hard work were part of her life. She knew how to use both to settle her mind.

She pushed herself, in an attempt to absolve the guilt that ate at her insides. She shoved the pitchfork through the straw bedding, then tossed it onto the growing pile in the wheelbarrow.

Her muscles adjusted to the rhythm of the work, but she was no closer after finishing the job than she had been to acquitting herself of the guilt.

Matt had a right to do his job. If circumstances had

been different, she'd probably offer to help him, but circumstances weren't different.

He believed in what he was trying to do, just as she believed in what she had to do. The knowledge filled her with a fresh wave of guilt . . . and shame.

Her conscience continued to heckle her long after she had showered away the afternoon's dirt.

In her office, she drummed her fingers on her desk, the bookkeeping awaiting her attention untouched. She had planned on spending the evening filling out the quarterly reports. Her good intentions never got past first base. Matt's face kept superimposing itself over the figures.

Her attention strayed to the bunch of sunflowers she'd stuffed into a mason jar. They carried the scent of late summer and were a reminder of the meadow where she and Matt had discovered the sheep. With that, her thoughts went full circle.

When Uncle Ray found her there, she was no closer to absolving herself than she had been hours ago. He set a cup of coffee in front her, the aroma as delicious as perfume.

She sniffed appreciatively. "Thanks."

"What is it that troubles you?" he asked.

"Nothing."

His eyes reproved her. "You will tell me when the time is right." Steady as a mountain and about as talkative, her uncle had been her anchor for more than twenty years, never pushing, but always there. "When you find your tongue, you will come to me."

Rebecca was grateful that he didn't pursue the subject. She knew him well enough to recognize that Uncle Ray would hold his tongue until he felt Rebecca was ready to talk. He had an uncanny sense of timing that she'd had cause again and again to appreciate.

When she was ready to talk, Uncle Ray would be there, just as he had been when she'd been a small child—a quiet presence that had held the family together when all else threatened to rip it apart.

The story came out in bits and pieces.

"I tried to persuade Matt to abandon his job," Rebecca finished. Shamed washed over her at the memory.

There were no words of reproach, only a quiet squeezing of her shoulder. "You will find a way to make it right." His smile came as a slow benediction. "Crow is sweetened when the words come from the heart."

Despite Uncle Ray's encouragement, Rebecca couldn't shake off her guilt. She'd disappointed Matt. More, she'd disappointed herself. It mattered, she discovered, mattered too much, what he thought of her, how he looked at her.

He mattered too much.

It was a sobering realization, one she wasn't comfortable admitting, but there it was.

She owed him an apology and wasn't going to get any work done until she'd made it.

Crow was a bitter dish to swallow, and admitting that she'd been in the wrong was the bitterest of all. It wasn't a position she was accustomed to occupying and it left her with a bad taste in her mouth.

Though it was nearing dusk, she went to the barn and saddled Maggie.

The air thinned as she and Maggie climbed the ridge which separated her place from the McCall spread. Wolves prowled the shadows for food. Their despondent cries went straight to her heart. Even though the scavengers raided her flocks, she had sympathy for their battle for survival.

Rebecca reined in the mare slightly as they approached Matt's cabin. She needed time to compose herself. The endless sky both surrounded and soothed.

The night would soon be thick and black, emphasizing the brilliance of the stars. In the city, the stars were frequently lost in the glitter of lights. Here, nothing interfered with the night's splendor.

She shook off the doubts that had pestered her during the ride and deliberately recalled Uncle Ray's words: *Crow is sweetened when the words come from the heart.*

She found Matt on the cabin porch working on his laptop by lantern light. She took her time, looped Maggie's reins over the post. He didn't look up, didn't acknowledge her presence in any way.

She planted herself in front of him and prepared to wait out his silence.

When he finally looked up, his eyes were shadowed with something akin to pain, or maybe it was disappointment.

"I was wrong." She swallowed over the lump of her conscience. "I had no right to try to talk you out of doing what you believe is right."

His eyes were wary, she noted. She didn't blame him.

"Was there something else you wanted?" he asked in a remote voice. "Thinking about offering me a bribe if I'll abandon my job?"

She supposed she deserved that and felt a slow flush stain her face. "I'm sorry." The apology came more easily than she'd anticipated. His nod prompted her to add, "I shouldn't have asked you to turn your back on your job." A fresh wave of guilt washed over her at what she'd done, and she turned to leave.

A hand on her arm stopped her.

The coldness in his eyes vanished, and his gaze softened. "I was wrong too."

She turned to him in surprise.

"I know you'd never bribe me or anyone. You've got too much integrity for that. You were fighting for what you believe. I'd do the same."

"Thanks." The word came out raggedly, and she cleared her throat. She didn't deserve to be let off the hook so easily.

"I respect someone who fights for what he—or she—believes in."

Just like that, they were back on even ground. Friends. She tested the word, knew that it was right. They *were* friends. She hadn't expected it, hadn't been looking for it.

The rancher and the naturalist. Whatever else happened, or didn't happen, between them, they were friends.

He took her hand, lacing her fingers through his.

She looked at their linked hands, each strong, each bearing the marks of hard work.

He stroked the sensitive skin on the underside of her wrist. Could he feel the jerk of her pulse at his touch?

"I can't change what I have to do," he said, "but I do understand what you're facing. Maybe, together, we can find a way to save the wolves and the ranchers."

She heard a new tone in his voice, something softer, as if he cared about her, not just as one of the ranchers who opposed him, but as a woman.

A breeze rippled over them, and she shivered. Her gaze met and tangled with his. For the span of a heartbeat, a single, endless moment, time ground to a standstill.

She felt a prickling at the nape of her neck. It was as if every sense was attuned to this man, this moment in time.

Small tremors shimmered down her spine. She'd

never experienced a reaction like this to any man—
instant awareness and the feeling that she'd stumbled
into something just beyond her grasp.

"You're cold," he said.

"Not anymore," she whispered.

He urged her closer until they were but a heartbeat
apart.

How long they stayed there, she didn't know, didn't
care. A sigh shuddered from her.

"I know why you fight so hard to protect your land,"
he said, after long moments had passed.

She turned her gaze toward the horizon. "I don't own
it. No one does. We only keep it in trust."

He lowered his head, then touched his lips to her
mouth.

She took a deep, steadying breath, willing her heart
to slow its pounding. Surely he could hear it, feel it, see
it. She raised her head, and her gaze slammed into his.

He continued to hold her, and she wasn't inclined to
put an end to it. There was something solid about him
that made her feel safe. Without warning, he released
her, but his gaze still held her captive.

She tried to discern the conflicting emotions she read
in his eyes, but a shutter had descended over his eyes.
One moment, she thought she might be on the brink of
discovery of Matt McCall, the man; the next, she knew
she had lost the opportunity. His jaw settled, his eyes
went flat, and she knew the battle was over.

Rebecca frowned a little as she watched him, wondering if she would ever really know him. She knew that there was much of him beneath the surface, parts that he would want to keep from her. Her instincts told her to explore, to dig, to understand.

Her instincts also told her that he wasn't going to make it easy for her.

Chapter Five

"**S**teady," Matt crooned to a tawny colored wolf. In the week since the wolves had arrived, he'd spent every available moment coaxing the wary animals to accept him and to allow him to tag them.

The humane cages holding the wolves allowed Matt to get close to the animals while still permitting them a certain amount of movement. The Akela Foundation hadn't spared any expense in designing the cages. Lightweight yet sturdy, they were easily set up and taken apart.

He hadn't seen Rebecca for a couple of days. He didn't know whether to be grateful or disappointed. Both, he decided. He missed their sparring even while he welcomed a break from her disturbing presence.

She was a fascinating combination of toughness and

vulnerability. The reality of her was too unsettling for his peace of mind.

Reluctantly, he smiled. He liked the lady. She fought for what she believed. Not many men would have stood up to him the way she had, but she was also totally a woman. She was that rare combination of guts and femininity.

He was taking it slow as he went about the process of tagging the wolves. The tags, no bigger than a grain of rice, had been developed by the scientists at the Foundation. Implanted in the animals' ears, the tags could only be read with a handheld scanner.

It was important to get the wolves to tolerate at least one person so that the tag could be checked and recorded at a future date. Also, if an animal were sick or injured, it would need human help.

The wolf, whom he'd named Goldie, maintained a cautious distance whenever he approached. She'd allowed him to touch her only once.

Time was on his side, time and determination.

Now, he adopted the soft, soothing tones he used with any animal. "You're a beautiful lady. But you already know that, don't you?"

Goldie lifted her head as if in confirmation.

Matt continued the one-sided conversation, all the while keeping a wary eye on the animal. Wolves, even ones accustomed to humans, were unpredictable creatures.

Goldie was the omega, the lowest-ranked member of

the pack. Wolves were social animals, with clearly defined ranking. The alpha male dominated all other members of the pack.

He inched his way closer and managed to pat Goldie's neck. To his astonishment, the animal didn't back off but stood still while he ran his hand down her back.

"See? It's not so bad. Pretty soon you might even like it." He chanced another pat on the powerful neck. "Good girl." Satisfied with the day's work, he backed off. He could undo all his progress by pushing too hard, too fast.

In the last few weeks, he'd managed to transport a half dozen wolves as well as tag some of those already there. He'd achieved an uneasy truce with most of the ranchers as he set about doing his job.

He was under no illusion that they liked or condoned what he was doing. Maybe, in time, he could find a way to earn their respect, if not their approval.

Several of the wolves had already been turned out on the range, the ones that had allowed him to get close enough to implant the identifying tags in their necks.

Goldie, more nervous than most, was a different matter. It would take days, maybe weeks, to get her to the point where she'd trust him enough. Until now, he was content to build the relationship between them.

So far, the wily Santanna eluded every attempt to capture and tag him, but Matt wasn't giving up. Santanna didn't know it, but he was going to be tagged along with the other wolves. As part of the relocation program, it was necessary to tag the wolves that already made their home in the plateaus of southern Colorado.

A lizard scuttled between Goldie's paws, causing her to bare her teeth.

Matt had a healthy respect for the deadly incisors which could rip and shred flesh all too easily.

Despite stories to the contrary, wolves rarely attacked humans, but Goldie was still skittish after the long trip from Canada. It didn't pay to take chances.

Careful to keep his movements casual, Matt stepped out of the way. "Easy," he soothed. "No one's going to hurt you."

He heard a sharp whoosh of relief. For a second, he thought the shuddering breath was his own before realizing it had come from behind him. Without turning, he knew it was Rebecca.

As slowly as possible, so as to not further upset the startled animal, he backed out of the cage and locked it behind him.

"Do you know what could have happened?" She walked toward him, hands fisted on her hips.

"Nothing happened."

"*This* time."

He was about to tell him that he could take care of himself when he realized it was concern, not anger, that had darkened her eyes to molten gold.

"She's a wild animal," she said. "Forget that and you could get hurt. Or worse."

"I'm not likely to forget, but we're becoming friends. Aren't we?" he asked Goldie.

The wolf had settled down, the stench of her fear tapering off in the fresh air.

He directed his attention back to Rebecca. Her eyes held a wary assessment. He didn't know whether it was aimed at himself or at Goldie.

"You shouldn't be working with her alone." She gestured to the skittish animal.

"I have a job to do."

"No one works with wild animals without backup. It's common sense."

"I don't need—"

"I was brought up on this land. I've seen what can happen to someone who gets in the way of a spooked wolf. It's not pretty. If she'd bitten you . . ."

"I'm no fool."

"Not a fool," she agreed easily. "But when a person's totally involved in what he's doing, he may take chances he wouldn't ordinarily take."

He wanted to throw her words back at her, but he couldn't. She was right. He had been caught up in her work, not paying sufficient attention to his surroundings. If he had, he might have seen the lizard and guessed at its effect on Goldie.

"You're right."

She looked surprised at his easy agreement. "I don't want anything happening to you."

"I didn't know you cared."

The corners of her mouth tipped upward. Could she be fighting a smile? "Let's just say you've grown on me."

After returning from Matt's place, Rebecca rubbed down Maggie, frowning over the lather the mare had worked up during their ride. Rebecca had pushed them both hard in an effort to try to come to terms with her feelings for Matt.

For the most part, she was content with her life, with her work. But every now and then, something or someone would come along and remind her of how lonely she really was. It was those times, like now, when she would have given almost anything to be held in a man's strong arms.

She liked him, genuinely liked him, something she hadn't felt for a man in more years than she cared to remember, but his job kept coming between them.

She skipped lunch, preferring the solitude of her office. She'd grab a sandwich later. Wearily, she rubbed the back of her neck. Tension coiled the tendons there into knots.

A smile chased the shadows from her face as she remembered that tomorrow was Saturday. The kids were coming.

Before then, she had a mountain of reports to wade through. She was the first to admit that paperwork was far down on her list of priorities, but she couldn't afford to neglect it.

She forced her attention back to the monthly report.

The ranch was operating in the black—by a slim margin. No matter how she juggled the figures, though, there was no way she could afford to hire a foreman.

Rebecca kept at it for another hour, paying bills and balancing the books. At last, she shoved her chair back and stood. The hours of inactivity had stiffened her muscles. She opened the French doors leading to the patio and allowed herself to dream of carrying out what her parents had started so many years ago.

They'd worked to keep alive the traditions of the tribal art. It had been on a trip to the reservation when they'd had the accident that had claimed their lives.

To honor them, Rebecca brought several children to the ranch every Saturday. There they learned the crafts of their ancestors, and, she hoped, a sense of their history.

It was with that in mind that she prepared the art materials for tomorrow when the children were due to arrive. Sorting through the colored sands, delicate feathers, and the other supplies she had purchased on the Internet, she put together enough kits for a half dozen children.

When a tribal elder delivered the children the following day, Rebecca was ready. She ushered the children into the great room of the house where she had the kits spread out on a long table.

After showing examples from her own modest collection of art to the children, she left them to it. She circulated between the mini-artists, offering encouragement and praise.

"Let your imagination soar," Rebecca said to a small girl with dark eyes and dark braids.

"Like this?" Sarah Runningbuck showed her rendition of an eagle in flight.

Rebecca smiled approvingly at the traditional design of bold colors and shapes. "You have the makings of a real artist."

Sarah raised her gaze to Rebecca's. "Do you really think so?"

Rebecca patted the small shoulder. "I sure do. Look how you've taken to it. You're a natural." She swallowed around the tightness in her throat as she watched Sarah's uncoordinated fingers grip the pastel chalk more firmly.

Sarah worked on her drawing diligently, all the while keeping up a continual stream of excited chatter.

"Can I do another?" she asked when she completed her picture.

"You bet."

Rebecca looked at the rapt expression on her small face. It was one of pure joy. She knew Sarah had experienced more heartache than most adults, let alone eight-year-olds, had to face in a lifetime. Yet she faced each challenge with a dogged determination that Rebecca couldn't help but admire.

Rebecca had been hosting these Saturday afternoon art lessons for handicapped children for over a year now, but the children's delight in the simple act of drawing made each time seem like the first.

It hadn't been easy, convincing the tribal elders to let her bring the children to the ranch. At first, Rebecca had been allowed to take only one child. Now, she routinely brought six to eight children there every Saturday.

They continued the art lesson for another hour. Judging that Sarah and the others had had enough for today, Rebecca callcd a halt to the instruction.

"Do we have to stop?" Sarah asked, lower lip jutting out.

" 'Fraid so, sweetie. But you'll be back next week. If you feel like it, you can take a ride on Maggie."

"Can I really?"

Ben walked up at that moment. "If Rebecca says so, then you can count on it."

"I think we've got a first-rate artist here," Rebecca said, giving the little girl a final hug.

"Sure looks like it," Ben said. "C'mon, Sarah. You and Maggie have a date in the corral."

Rebecca watched as Ben pushed the wheelchair out the French doors and over the uneven ground to the corral where he helped her mount the docile Maggie.

She loved each of the kids who'd participated in the program, but there was something special about Sarah. Though their circumstances were different, they'd each known loss.

When Rebecca had first met Sarah, the little girl was afraid of her own shadow. Now she was a regular at the ranch.

Rebecca's only regret was that she hadn't started the program years earlier. Children from the reservation faced a lifetime of doors being closed to them. She had determined that expressing themselves in art, finding the joy of creating, wouldn't be one of those doors.

Her parents had started the program shortly before their death. It had taken Rebecca nearly two decades to bring their dream to life again.

At first, it had been for them, to honor their memory. Now it was for herself. Working with the children, watching them create and learn filled an empty place inside her, but a vital part of her life was missing. That part longed for a partner, a helpmeet.

Sarah and the other children each took a turn on Maggie before the van arrived to take them back to the reservation.

Rebecca walked back to where Maggie was waiting patiently. "You were a real lady today," she said, patting the mare affectionately. She reached into her pocket and pulled out a piece of taffy.

Maggie whinnied her appreciation and chewed it noisily.

Rebecca started to lead the horse to the barn to rub her down when a voice halted her.

"That was something else." Matt leaned against the fence, one leg hooked under a rail, his face warm with admiration.

"How long have you been here?"

"Long enough."

Long enough for what?

"Long enough to see that you're a fraud," he answered her unspoken question.

"A fraud?"

"That's right. A fraud. You give a great performance, but inside, you're a marshmallow."

She'd been called a lot of things but never a marshmallow. She wasn't sure she liked it. In fact, she was fairly sure she didn't. "You want to explain that?"

"You know, a marshmallow. All hard and crusty on the outside and soft and gooey on the inside."

Not knowing how to answer that, she started toward the barn again.

Matt followed. "That was pretty wonderful what you did with that little girl."

She lifted the saddle and blanket from Maggie and began rubbing her down, her hands moving over the mare's sleek back in rhythmic circles. She kept her eyes averted, but she felt Matt's gaze on her.

"Why didn't you tell me?" he asked.

"I didn't know you'd be interested." It was a lame answer, but all she could come up with.

Matt placed his hands over hers, stilling them. "I think it's more than that. I think you were afraid I'd see something you didn't want me to."

"That's crazy." Shaking off his hands, she moved to Maggie's other side and repeated the process.

"Is it?"

She nodded, uncomfortable with the warmth in his eyes, in his voice. "Don't make me out to be something I'm not. Once a week, I bring some children out to the ranch and draw with them. Maybe take them for a ride." She picked up a curry comb and began grooming the horse.

"It takes a special lady to do what you're doing. To give up your Saturdays for a bunch of kids."

Impatient, she turned around and faced him. "There's nothing noble about it. The kids enjoy it, and so do I. That's all." She stopped. She had no call to talk to Matt that way. No call at all. He'd only been interested, and she'd turned her temper on him. "I'm sorry. It's just that—"

"You don't want people knowing about it."

"That's part of it, but not all. Plenty of people know what we're trying to do here. But I've tried to keep it low-key. If the newspapers got a hold of it, they'd be out here, taking pictures, turning it into some kind of sideshow and making the kids out to be freaks." She inhaled deeply. "They're normal kids who've had some tough breaks.

"That's what this is all about. It's showing them that they can—with a few limitations—do anything they want to."

Matt touched her arm. "Your secret's safe with me," he said, and sent her a warm glance that caused a catch in the back of her throat.

She looked at his clear eyes and knew he was telling

the truth. He could no more lie than he could turn her back on the wolves he was so determined to help.

"Thanks." Her voice was quiet now, softer, without the edge that had coated it moments ago. Her pulse leapt, then steadied when he circled her wrist with his fingers. She tried to concentrate on what he was saying rather than on the feelings he was rousing within her.

"You're welcome. Maybe someday you'd let me help you with them."

How many times had she wished for an extra pair of hands to help with the kids? Uncle Ray, Ben and the ranch hands helped when they could, but they were usually needed elsewhere if she were to keep the ranch a paying concern. "You'd do that?"

His nod was all the answer she needed.

She thought of the problems plaguing the reservations. Unemployment. Poverty. Alcoholism.

She'd been fortunate, but too many other Native American children hadn't received the advantages she had.

She'd never discussed her dream with anyone. Not even Uncle Ray. "I need to make the ranch a paying proposition. Right now, it's self-supporting, but only just."

"There's more, isn't there?"

"There's more. But it's not likely to happen so there's no point in discussing it."

He brought her hand to his lips. "There is if you want to make it come true." At her disbelieving look, he said, "You have to say the dream out loud. At least twenty times a day. That way, you start believing it can happen."

She'd never put words to her dream before. The idea frightened her, but it pulled at her as well. She suddenly wanted to say the words aloud, to test them. She looked at Matt and knew there was no one else with whom she'd rather share her dream.

"I want to turn the ranch into a place for children with disabilities. Full time." The words hung in the air. Both were silent, loathe to break the spell the words had cast.

"It'll take money," she said with a long sigh. "Lots of money. More than I could put together for a long time the way things are going right now."

"What would you need to start making the kind of money you'd need?"

"We'd have to breed more sheep, add more land."

"I wish you'd told me sooner," he murmured.

"What difference would it have made?"

"Maybe none. But at least I'd have understood." He uncurled his hand from hers and cupped her chin. "It's a great dream. You'll make it happen."

"You're a born optimist."

"No. I'm just someone who believes that dreams can come true. If you want something enough, you'll make it happen. Look at me. I finally got to do what I always wanted."

"You mean working with the wolves?"

"And using a degree that I earned more than a decade ago. It took me a while to get my priorities straight. Now that I have, I know I can't go back to riding a desk." He dipped his head to study Rebecca's face. "Your turn," he said.

She took her time before answering. "The reservation can be a good place. I spent a lot of time there when I was growing up. Uncle Ray took me. He wanted me to understand my roots. I made friends and had fun. But I always knew I could go home at the end of the day. I didn't have to stay there day after day, go to school there, wake up there and know there was nothing else."

"You make it sound pretty bleak."

"Too often it is."

"What about kids like Sarah?"

Her smile came quickly, her eyes warming to the color of rich honey. "Sarah was my first student. It was because of her that the tribal elders agreed to let other kids come."

He wondered if she knew how appealing she looked at that moment, her eyes filled with love and wonder as she talked about the children.

Something slow and tender unfurled in his chest. Some of what he was feeling must have shown in his eyes, for a slow blush worked its way up her neck to blossom on her cheeks. He followed its progress, amused when the color heightened as she realized that he had continued to stare at her.

"What's wrong with her?" He wanted to yank back the words as soon as they left his mouth. "Sorry. I didn't mean—"

"It's all right. Sarah knows she's different. She has cerebral palsy. Her mother has three other children. She does all she can do to keep her family together, especially after Sarah's father took off." Her smile widened. "Sarah's got a lot of spunk. She keeps all of us on our toes."

He wondered if she knew just how much she revealed about herself when she talked about the kids. There was no mistaking the compassion in her voice or the softening of her eyes. Her heart, he thought, was as big as the land with room enough for a bunch of kids from the reservation.

The different layers of feeling this woman generated in him took on a deeper texture. Respect, admiration, tenderness, and something else . . . something that he was loathe to identify.

"As long as I've already put my foot in my mouth, I have another question."

"You want to know why I didn't grow up on the reservation," she guessed.

He nodded in answer.

"My mother's family owned this property. It was deeded to her great-great-grandfather by the governor around the turn of the last century. Over the years, they built the place up."

His gaze took in the ranch house, white adobe with

a red tile roof. Low-slung and sprawling, it looked serene in its desert home, a perfect complement to its surroundings.

"You must love it."

"I do." She gave a grimace. "Even when it's my turn to muck out the barn."

He shrugged off his vest and rolled up his sleeves. "Now that I'm here, could you use a hand?"

She looked undecided, then nodded. She flashed him a smile and handed him a pitchfork.

He gave in to the urge to watch her as she worked. Something about her fascinated him. He was aware of the pungent scents of barn and animal that wafted through the open doors. Shafts of sunlight routed the shadows in the corners.

She wasn't afraid of getting her hands dirty. He liked that about her. He had a feeling there were a lot of things to like about Rebecca.

A wisp of dark hair fell across her face, and she pushed it back, giving him a clear view of profile. The high brow and slash of cheekbones bore testimony of her heritage, both complemented by the pale gold of her skin.

The sculpted line of her shoulders and back, together with the easy way she moved, hinted at a lifetime of hard work.

By the time they were finished, he was adding another piece to the whole that made up Rebecca. She wasn't too proud to accept help when it was offered, but neither would she ask for it. It was that mix of practicality and pride that made her a complex and intriguing woman.

"Thanks," she said, looking up.

Bits of straw clung to her hair. Without thinking, he reached out to brush them away. Even sweat-stained and dirty, she was breathtaking.

It was more than the fact that she had hair that reminded him of a raven's wing and deep gold eyes. It was more basic than her staggering looks. Her love of the land, her reluctance to see the wolves destroyed despite the fact that they were costing her her livelihood, all touched something deep within him.

The air hummed with tension.

Matt forced himself to tear his gaze away from her and focused on the rough hewn beams of the barn. Darkened with age, they were silent reminders of a rugged era, of the men and women who'd struggled to survive during that time.

He admired her face in the slats of sunlight. Unapologetically angled, it was not beautiful in a conventional sense. Her features were too strong, too compelling for mere prettiness.

No, her face would never be termed pretty, but it was appealing in a way that invited the viewer to take a second, and a third, look. It hinted at the strength that was so much a part of her.

It was her eyes, though, that captivated him. Eyes that saw everything and mirrored more than she believed. Eyes that could warm to honey as she gazed at the children from the reservation or darken to the color of old gold when she was angry.

At the moment, they settled on him with breathtaking intensity. What he saw there caused him to draw in a sharp breath.

He took another deep breath, then expelled it in another deliberately controlled exhalation.

He reached out, pushed back a stray strand of hair which had escaped the band.

Red flared briefly on her high-set cheekbones.

He gave into impulse and touched his lips to hers. The kiss, which he'd intended only as a light peck, stretched into seconds, then into minutes. He rested his hands at her waist.

When his lips had met hers, he knew his imagination hadn't equaled reality. His every thought, every feeling had focused on the feel of her lips beneath his.

Rebecca kissed the same way she did everything— withholding nothing, giving everything.

When he released her, he was trembling. "That was—"

"Incredible."

Incredible. He couldn't argue with that. Had the earth moved? Or had it simply been the pounding of his heart that made him think the world had shifted?

Rebecca put a finger to her lips. To still their trembling? he wondered. "Care to play hooky with me tomorrow? I think we could both use a day off from work."

Still reeling from the kiss, he could only nod. He said an awkward good-bye.

Three hours later, Matt e-mailed his daily report to the Akela Foundation, but his mind was far away from the migration patterns of wolves.

He thought about Rebecca's patience with the little girl. She'd shown a side of herself he'd never seen, not that it surprised him. He'd known nearly from the first meeting that she wasn't as hard and tough as she pretended. She was caring and understanding, warm and generous.

She'd been uncomfortable with him witnessing her work with the children. He smiled, remembering how she'd guided Sarah's hand with the paints. Her hands had lingered on Sarah's shoulders as Rebecca had knelt in front of the wheelchair to whisper something to the little girl.

All her reserve and cool politeness melted away when she was with the kids. An unreasonable jealousy arose within him.

He shook his head. Jealous over a bunch of kids. He had it bad.

Like it or not, he cared about her.

Rebecca was a complex woman with as many sides as there were colors in the sky at sunset. Drawn by the idea of observing another of the spectacular Colorado sunsets, he stepped outside. No pastels here. Vivid bands of color striped the sky. Bold colors, contrasting with each other, but making a perfect whole—like the woman who increasingly occupied his thoughts.

The evening sounds of the desert broke the silence. The scuffling of a small animal burrowing into the ground, the caw of a crow, the shrill call of mating insects, each distinct, each necessary in the order of nature.

He let his mind wander, imagining hc could hear another sound—the sound of Rebecca's voice praising the little girl. It was a sound he'd never forget.

Matt tried to picture Rebecca as a child. She had probably been a tad serious, with questioning eyes and a smile that peeked out at unexpected moments. He liked the image.

He could also picture the children she'd have—small girls and boys with dark hair and solemn eyes. She'd be a good mother.

Image after image crowded his mind, and he shook his head to dispel them.

Rebecca Whitefeather was the last woman with whom he should get involved. She was opinionated, mulish, and all together exasperating.

A small voice inside his head reminded him that she was also intelligent, lovely, and compassionate. And that was what bothered him most of all.

Chapter Six

Rebecca loved mornings.

She always had, though she rarely took the time to watch the way the sun painted the sky with color and verve. Now she breathed in the early morning air and filled her lungs with the sweet scent of it.

It was a stolen day, one of those rare mornings when she could play hooky.

Working the land was her livelihood and her love. It was something she'd always done and would always do, not simply because it was necessary but because it was a part of her as surely as her Navajo blood.

As much as she loved it, though, she also treasured time away from the ever-present chores and constant demands. The desert had to constantly be beat back, or it would overrun the cleared yard and fields.

She wondered what Matt thought of his adopted home, if he might decide to settle here permanently.

Maybe, just maybe, he was beginning to feel something for her. A smile tugged at her lips as she considered the possibility. Her invitation to spend the day with her had been an impulse. Now she was glad that she had followed through with it.

Pleasurable anticipation curled through her at the idea of sharing the day with Matt. Inevitably, her thoughts strayed to yesterday's kiss. It had been a long time since she'd felt so feminine and cherished.

Rebecca handed an apple to Maggie, who gobbled it down as Matt arrived.

He dismounted and joined her. "You spoil her."

She raised a brow. "I suppose you don't spoil Trapper."

"You got me." Crinkles at the corners of his eyes gave away his silent laughter.

As though aware that he was the topic of conversation, Trapper snorted and pranced about.

Matt patted the big gelding's neck. "I know, boy. You don't like to be kept waiting, do you?" He flashed Rebecca a teasing smile. "That's what happens when you're taking out a lady."

He gave Rebecca a boost up on Maggie, then mounted Trapper, whispering to the gelding in a conspiratorial manner.

Rebecca could have sworn the horse nodded in agreement.

She kept the pace slow so that they could appreciate the scenery. Colorado columbine bloomed in unexpected places, their flowers spots of brilliant color against the sun-seared ground. In spite of the drought, the land held its own kind of beauty, one filled with stark contrasts. The sky, as though to make up for the arid ground, was a vivid blue.

As though aware of her resolve that this be a day to remember, Matt proved to be an agreeable companion. By unspoken agreement, they avoided the topic of the wolves. She feared their differences would always separate them, but for now, she was content to enjoy the rare harmony between them.

Today belonged to the two of them. There'd be time enough later to worry over all that divided them.

She showed him a secluded canyon, a ragged gash in the mountainside made by a stream that had tumbled over boulders millions of years ago. The only remaining evidence of the ancient river were fossils imprinted into the rock walls now painted a rich pallette of colors by the sun.

Rusty-red boulders stood as sentinels at the mouth of the canyon. She showed him markings on the canyon walls, the writings of an ancient people. It was a land that time had forgotten.

When the ground grew rough, she slowed the pace even more, mindful of the dry ground pockmarked with cavities and fissures. The feisty Maggie didn't like slowing the pace, even when the going got rough.

Rebecca shared with him the special places. The red sand-drifts that provided the backdrop for magnificent rock formations. The cactus gardens where pines spiraled upward and were a dark green, contrasting with the silvery green mesquite.

She thought how comfortable she was with him, how right it felt to show one of her favorite parts of the world to him.

"It's never the same, is it?" Matt asked. "And yet always the same."

She understood what he meant and was gratified that his feelings so closely matched her own. She pointed to a flat overhang of rock which provided a welcome bit of shade. "Time for lunch."

Matt hobbled the horses while she opened her saddlebags and spread out the picnic lunch.

He looked at the array of food and whistled. "You've got enough here to feed an army."

"We could share with Maggie and Trapper," she said, tongue in cheek.

"No way. They've got their own food."

She followed his gaze to where the horses chomped on the grain Matt had brought for them.

Rebecca poured lemonade from a thermos into paper cups and handed one to him.

He finished it in one gulp and held out his cup for more. "I didn't know anyone still made fresh-squeezed lemonade any more."

"I do. For special occasions." She spoke without

thinking and then wondered what he made of her words.

They feasted on cold roast beef sandwiches. "Now for dessert." She rubbed an apple against her sleeve and handed it to him.

His tongue curled as the tart juice slid over it. "It's good," he said between bites.

"There's nothing better than a just-picked apple." An apple crunched under her teeth.

By the time they'd finished, Matt was making a show of patting his stomach. "You keep feeding me like this and I'll get a paunch."

She looked at his flat stomach that boasted not an ounce of extra flesh. "Since you feel like you need the exercise, I'll let you clean up."

He gave her a pained look. "Thanks." When he had finished, he turned to her. One long stride ate up the distance between them. He was now but a heartbeat away.

She drew in a quick breath when he laid his palm on her cheek. His hand had developed callouses over the last weeks. She liked the feel of his work-roughened hand on her skin.

Rebecca began an exploration of her own, trailing her fingers across the hard line of his jaw, the tiny cleft in his chin, the strong column of his throat, where a pulse quickened its beat.

His very look seemed a caress, and she flushed under the warmth of it. A slow, sure smile appeared upon his lips, quickening her pulse. She moistened suddenly dry lips and swallowed.

When he lowered his head, she guessed his intent. She could have objected, could have moved. She did neither. Instead, she waited for the kiss she knew would make the world stop.

His hands crept infinitesimally upward until his fingers came in contact with the sensitive skin of her upper arms. She shivered tremulously at his touch and felt her stomach muscles contract painfully. He could not possibly be unaware of her reaction, but he gave no notice of it, except to tighten his hold of her ever so slightly.

He brushed his lips against her hair, along her cheek, until they found hers. He let the kiss linger. He tasted of lemonade, a mixture of sweet and tart, and she gave herself up to the pleasure of his warm mouth pressed to hers.

Stars didn't explode inside her head. It wasn't that kind of kiss. It was sweet, tentative, asking . . . seeking, for what she wasn't sure.

One beat of her heart tripped madly over the next, the rhythm picking up and destroying her short-lived confidence. She felt strange, shimmery, and very much alive. All because a man had kissed her. Not just any man, she silently amended. One man in particular.

She gave and, in giving, received. The kiss changed, and then there were stars. Bright, glittering stars that touched something deep inside her. It was every woman's dream. More, it was *her* dream.

She sighed once, then again, a soft ripple of sound in the waning afternoon.

There was only the two of them. Her head resting in the indent of his shoulder, she was aware of only him and the attraction humming between them.

For the moment, she forgot their differences over the wolves. All she knew was that for one wonderful moment, she was being held in strong, masculine arms.

She put a hand to her heart, surprised to feel its steady rhythm. Surely such a kiss would have destroyed its even beat as surely as it had her composure.

The world didn't just stop at his kiss; it tilted off its axis before coming to that stop. She risked a glance at him. Her only consolation was that he appeared nearly as flumoxed as she did.

Though the kiss had ended, Matt was still achingly aware of her. A strand of hair teased her cheek, and he reached out to smooth it back in place. The feel of her skin, as velvety as a summer night, nearly undid him.

She'd kissed him like she meant it.

His chest felt as though it had been seized by a powerful fist. He tried to breathe, but her scent filled his head, clouded his senses.

The lady was a witch, a sorceress, an enchantress. Whatever name he gave her, though, he knew she was dangerous. She threatened his resolve, his determination to complete his job.

He didn't need the complication of a woman in his life, especially a woman like Rebecca, who would demand more than he had to give. He'd known her little more than a few weeks, but she'd already upset his carefully-ordered existence.

He looked up to find her eyes on him, wide and questioning. He took her hand, urging her down to the blanket.

She stretched out, using her jacket to pillow her head.

Most women wouldn't be content to spend the day under the scorching sun with nothing more exciting planned than scouting for a place for transplanted wolves, but then Rebecca wasn't most women. He was beginning to accept that. It pleased him. It also scared him.

His contemplation was cut short with her next words. "Tell me about your family."

The air whooshed out of him. He didn't usually talk about his family, except for his grandfather. So why was he tempted to share part of himself with Rebecca?

He avoided looking directly at her and stared up at the sky. Was that a cloud? Rain would be an answer to the ranchers' prayers.

He shifted his gaze and spotted a small lizard just as it scuttled out from underneath a rock. Just as quickly it took refuge under another one.

Rebecca remained silent, as though sensing his need to think through whatever he might say.

He was grateful for the time. What did he feel about his parents after all these years? He'd like to be able to say that he didn't feel a thing, but that would be a lie.

He thought about all the years he'd felt driven to defend his mother, to downplay her desertion. With Rebecca, though, he no longer felt compelled to gloss over the truth. "My mother left when I was nine years old." He made a sound that was not quite a laugh. "She left her husband, her son, her home without a backward glance."

"Why?"

Matt heard the confusion in Rebecca's voice. For a long time, he'd been equally confused. Closely on the heels of that came guilt. He'd blamed himself, wondering what he'd done to make his mother leave without so much as a good-bye. If he'd been more obedient, if he'd made his bed every day, if he'd been less trouble, would she have stayed?

The questions had tormented him for years until his grandfather had taken him aside and told him the truth. His mother had left her family because she was selfish. By then, Matt had convinced himself that he didn't care.

An echo reached him across the distance of more than two decades. Words that were etched in his brain, engraved on his heart. He'd been only nine at the time, crouched in the hallway, listening to yet another of his mother's diatribes. He'd wanted to run and hide, to cover his ears from the venom that spilled forth from the people who'd given birth to him.

He had heard the same ugly words hurled back and forth many times, but this was the first time he'd understood the depth of his mother's hatred, not only for her husband but for her son as well.

"She thought my father could give her everything. For a while, it worked. Then he became more and more successful. She wanted, needed, his attention. By that time, his business had taken off and he didn't have the time to give her what she needed."

"What about you?"

"What about me?"

"She must have cared about you." Rebecca didn't pry. She simply waited him out.

"She tried. In her own way. By the time she left, my parents ended up strangers living in the same house."

A coldness had wrapped itself around his heart the day his mother had walked out and had disappeared.

He was annoyed at Rebecca, angry at the way she'd gotten him to remember things better left in the past. He met her gaze, and the empathy in her eyes sucked the annoyance right out of him.

She saw him, saw through him, as no one else ever had. Something stirred deep within him, and, for the space of a heartbeat, he wanted her to be part of his life. Forever.

Transfixed, he stared at her, so aware of her that he wondered she didn't feel the intensity of his gaze.

He'd kept his voice emotionless, but it didn't stop the tears from welling up in Rebecca's eyes. He saw them and wished he had never started the story, but it was too late to stop.

"How long has she been gone?"

He was silent, minute turning into minute. When he answered, it was with remembered pain. "Nearly twenty-five years."

Certainly, it had been long enough for him to get over his mother's desertion. What he'd never been able to forget, though, was his own guilt that it had been his fault.

Rebecca reached out and covered his hand with her own. Her fingers wrapped around his, a wordless gesture of comfort that touched him more than the simple touch should warrant. For long minutes, they stayed that way, neither feeling the need to speak.

At last, he pulled his hand away. He heard Rebecca's murmur of disappointment, but when he looked up, her eyes were filled with compassion, not the pity he halfway expected.

"I'm sorry," she said. "Sorry that it hurt you so much."

He started to deny that he'd been hurt and then stopped himself. The simplicity of her words loosened the restraint he'd always felt whenever he talked about his mother.

"I learned a lot." Like never letting anyone get too close. Like keeping his feelings to himself. He couldn't bear to see the distress in her eyes. "I'm a big boy now."

"What about your father?"

"After my mother left, he put everything into the business. It became even more successful." And he, Matt, became even more alone.

Rebecca skimmed a hand down his cheek.

He wasn't accustomed to sympathy, didn't know how to deal with it.

"Do you ever see your mother?" she asked.

"I call her on her birthday and Christmas." He winced at the cold disinterest in his voice and shrugged. "I'm not good at the relationship thing."

"How do you know?"

"She tells me that every time we talk."

"Well, that proves it," Rebecca said with tart asperity. "You're hopeless. Your mother ought to know since she's such an expert on healthy relationships."

Matt was stunned into silence, then gave a sound that was not quite a laugh. "I never thought of it that way."

"As an adult?"

"Yeah."

Rebecca had managed to turn what he knew to be true upside down. He didn't like it. Not one bit. So his voice was sharper than he intended when he said, "It was a long time ago."

She didn't look put off at his curt tone. "Not that long."

She was right. He could still remember the bewilderment, the pain, the guilt he'd felt that day when his mother stood by the front door with bags packed and a frown in her eyes. His father's gruff words had only added to Matt's confusion and hurt.

"I wanted them to love me as much as I loved them, but I gave up on that before I turned ten." He had closed himself off from others at the same time.

"What about Amos?"

Grateful for the change of subject, Matt smiled in memory. "He was great. I didn't get to see him as much as I'd have liked, but I knew he cared." He found himself telling her about his grandfather and his part in killing the wolves more than a half a century ago. It was important that she understand how much this meant to Matt himself, to Amos's memory.

From there, it seemed only natural to tell her of his father's lack of business ethics and why he, Matt, had decided to leave the family business. "I couldn't be a part of it," he finished. "Not when I found out what he was doing."

"You'd never do anything unethical."

Her steadfast trust moved him in a way that little in his life ever had, and he realized that she had an uncanny way of clipping him behind the knees with her implicit faith in him.

He also realized he'd told her more about himself and his family than he had ever shared with anyone. The thought left him uncomfortable. "Enough about me. Tell me about you."

She lifted a shoulder. "My parents died when I was seven."

"It couldn't have been easy," he said, watching her face.

"No. Not easy. But I have lots of memories."

"Were your parents in love?" Without knowing why, he knew that her answer was important.

"Very much. Dad used to brush Mom's hair every night. Said he liked the way it fell past her shoulders onto her back." Rebecca touched her own hair. "She was fair. I always wanted to have blonde hair like hers, but I take after my dad."

Matt smoothed his hand down the river of her hair. "Your hair's beautiful. It's the first thing I noticed about you."

"When Uncle Ray came to take care of me, he tried braiding it. After a week, we both decided it'd be better if I wore it straight."

Matt chuckled at the picture her words conjured up. "I like your uncle."

"He thinks you have potential."

He snorted out a laugh. "I'd think I'd be the last person to be on his good side."

"Uncle Ray sees beyond what is now."

"You sound like him."

She smiled at him, genuine pleasure lighting her face. "That's the nicest thing you could have said."

"You love him a lot." He made a statement of the words.

Her nod said it all.

He knew a sharp pang of envy before pushing it aside. Love wasn't something with which he'd had a lot of experience. He'd known companionship, but never love.

Even before she'd left, his mother hadn't had time for all the extra things a child needs and wants. Things like bedtime stories followed by a kiss to scare away the bogeyman, cookies and milk in the afternoon, a soothing touch to bandage a skinned knee, a soft word to heal hurt feelings.

Matt thought about some of the kids he'd met through Rebecca's weekend art program and realized he'd been lucky. Even without love, he'd had a home— of sorts. Many of the kids Rebecca worked with didn't even have that, but were wards of the state with no one and no place to call their own.

He'd made it, but sometimes, in the dark hours before night slipped into day, he still wished for . . . He shook his head, impatient with the feelings that even two decades hadn't been able to vanquish.

He found Rebecca looking at him with understanding warming her eyes and flushed. The last thing he wanted was pity.

"Is there someone special in your life?" he asked, and was surprised that it mattered, that he cared if she were in a relationship of any kind.

"Not anymore," she said. "I was engaged once. It didn't work out."

"What happened?"

Her face took on a pensive look. "He didn't understand how much working with the kids from the reservation meant to me. He ended up giving me an
ultimatum—them or him." She shrugged. "I chose the
kids."

"His loss."

"Yeah. That's what I thought."

Matt didn't bother analyzing why he felt so relieved
at the news.

They were quiet now. It was a good kind of silence.
The kind that gave a person room to think, to feel. She
didn't fill it with chatter as many women would. She
seemed content to simply share the moment with him.

He looked down at her, a smile touching his lips. Her
eyes were closed, her face tilted up to catch the sun.
She looked like summer with her face flushed from the
sun and her hair straight as rain.

She smelled of sunshine and a faint, elusive scent
that reminded him of wild honeysuckle. She didn't
have a smidgin of makeup. She wore faded jeans and a
shirt that had seen better days. And she was the most
beautiful woman he'd ever known.

He took her hand and turned it over. Her nails were
short and unpolished, the skin work-roughened. "I've
always thought that you can tell a lot about a person by
her hands."

"What are you? A palm reader?"

"Uh-uh. A man who knows hard work when he sees

it." He stroked the faint ridges of callus along her palm. "And feels it."

"My work takes me outside most of the time." She eased her hand from his.

He saw the color ride high on her cheeks and guessed at its cause. "Don't be embarrassed. Your hands tell me you care about what you do."

She took his hand and traced the blisters he'd developed over the last weeks. "I guess we have something in common after all."

Though a small thing, the comparison startled him. Were he and Rebecca alike?

At one time he'd have denied it emphatically, but now, he wasn't so sure. She was committed to her job. So was he. She fought for what she believed. So did he. She loved the land. So did he.

The list went on until he was shaking his head. Abruptly, he pulled away.

Chapter Seven

They rode in near silence, only occasionally breaking it. Neither mentioned the kiss. Rebecca wondered what had caused Matt to break away from her so suddenly.

She shouldn't have let it bother her that he'd pulled away as though he'd been scalded, but it was too late for that, far too late. Like it or not, she cared about him. She was beginning to believe that she always would, and that caring was perilously close to loving.

It hurt her heart at what he'd revealed about his family, but even that did not hurt as much as the fact that he'd tried to hide it. It reminded her of the times she'd tried to hide her own pain after the death of her parents.

She'd been lucky. Though she'd lost both parents, she'd had Uncle Ray.

Shortly after the accident that had taken her parents,

he'd found her curled up in her closet crying. He had lifted her onto his lap and rocked her in his arms.

He hadn't tried to talk her out of her tears. Instead, he'd let her cry it out. Then he explained that her parents would always be with her because she carried them in her heart.

The simple lesson had remained with her, and though she had shed more tears, she no longer felt the aching loss.

Dusk was settling in. The sun started its slow descent, and the temperature dropped. At the same time, the wind picked up.

A change in the air had her stilling. Instinctively, she checked the sky. Time to start back home.

Matt followed her gaze where thunderclouds, with their underbelly of gunmetal gray, sulked over the horizon. "What—"

She waved him to silence, listening. She sensed the eve of the storm dancing in the air. "Rain's coming."

At that moment, Trapper pulled up short.

"I think there's something in his hoof," Matt said. He dismounted and hunkered down to check the gelding's hoof.

Rebecca dismounted as well, her uneasiness growing with every minute. The wind, silent until then, gave a bad-tempered bluster. "Is he all right?" She raised her voice as the wind snatched at it.

"He's picked up a stone," Matt said.

He'd barely finished getting out the words when

lightning fractured the sky. The landscape took on a surreal quality under the blue-white light.

Thunder roared over the squall of the wind, ricocheting off the mountains and canyon walls. Not to be outdone, the wind picked up even more, blustering angry hisses.

Matt was digging the stone from Trapper's hoof when lightning arced across the sky once more. The big gelding reared back, his hooves slicing the air.

"Easy, boy," Matt shouted. "It's only lightning. Nothing to get excited about."

The horse pawed the air, and Matt sidestepped, barely missing being struck by Trapper's hooves.

Rebecca rushed to help.

"Watch out," he shouted when she got too close.

Trapper, now thoroughly spooked by the bursts of thunder and lances of lightning, struck out again. Matt took a running leap, pushing Rebecca out of the way just as the horse's hooves would have struck her.

Suddenly the heavens opened up. Rain, not the gentle soaking she'd prayed for but a dense downpour, battered them.

She thought of the ranch and the animals. She had to get home. She grabbed for Maggie's reins, but the horse reared back sharply.

Rebecca edged closer. She reached for the reins but caught hold of the rope coiled on the saddle instead. Made on the reservation, the tightly woven hemp had a tensile-like strength. She made another try for the reins but slipped. With those few lost seconds, the mare eluded Rebecca's grasp.

Trapper disappeared into the darkness with Maggie close behind him.

Matt started after them.

"Don't bother," Rebecca said. "They're long gone." She blew her damp bangs from her face. "They'll be all right. I'm not so sure about us." A glint of metal caught her eye through the cauldron of rain and wind. She knew too well what that bit of metal meant. "Don't move," she yelled.

She heard the clank of metal against metal followed closely by his scream.

The trap had snapped shut.

"Hold on." She found a branch, wedged it between the jaws of the trap, and pushed with all her strength. Her muscles bunched with the effort. An icy rivulet of sweat trickled down between her shoulder blades as she thought of the damage the trap could do to a leg.

She glanced at Matt's face. Pain crossed his eyes and pulled at the corners of his mouth. Cords stood out in his neck, and he pressed his lips together.

The trap sprung open and he pulled out his leg.

She knelt beside him, and with infinite care, pulled off his boot. Fortunately, the heavy leather had spared him the worst of it. Still, blood had started to seep through the leg of his jeans. Using her pocket knife, she cut through the denim.

Despite the protection of his boot, the viscous teeth

of the trap had sliced through flesh with terrible efficiency.

Frantically, she searched for some way to treat the wound and recalled something Uncle Ray had told her long ago when she'd stumbled into a hornet's nest, and angry welts had raised on her arms and face.

To her amazement, he had smeared his hands with mud from a nearby puddle. "Mud can stop infection. Pack it over the wound and keep it wet."

The downpour had seeped into the earth, turning it to mud in a matter of minutes. She knelt and slathered the oozing mud over Matt's leg.

Even through the murky gray of the rain, she could make out the white lines of agony etched around his mouth. His breath came in short, sharp gasps that the steady pummeling of rain couldn't drown out.

She untied the bandanna from her neck and wrapped it around the wound, sealing the mud inside, then helped him pull on his boot.

"Is there some kind of shelter around here? An abandoned cabin? Anything?" he asked.

"There's a shepherd's cabin about two miles south. We can make it there if we follow the river." Panic crawled through her. With Matt's injury, she didn't think he'd make it on two feet. She pushed that from her mind.

"You can make it," he said. "I'm not going anywhere." He patted his leg. "Not with this."

"You can if you lean on me."

"I outweigh you by at least seventy pounds."

"So?"

He gave her an impatient look. "You'll never be able to take my weight."

"Let me decide what I can take. Are you going to sit around whining or are we going to get moving?"

His eyes narrowed. "Whining?"

She held his gaze with an unwavering one of her own. "That's what I said."

Slowly, he shook his head. "You're one heck of a woman, Rebecca Whitefeather."

"Save the flattery and give me your hand." He slipped his hand inside hers, and she helped him up. "Now, put your arm around my shoulders."

Matt did as she said, a good part of his weight shifting onto her. Her knees buckled. Only her quick reflexes kept them from landing face down in the mud.

"This isn't going to work," he growled.

"I need a minute." She pulled in air, hating the desperation in her voice, at the same time hoping he didn't hear it. She braced her legs and straightened. "Okay. Let's get going."

Out of necessity, they moved cautiously, picking their way over the uneven ground. As the rain grew heavier, they slowed their pace even more. Rivulets began to wend themselves over the unabsorbent land. Pools of water collected in depressions in the earth.

When she slipped, Matt caught her, but the effort

cost him. She could feel it as his body tensed against hers. Her knees felt like wet noodles, but she forced back the groan that sprang to her lips.

By mutual consent, they stopped in the shelter of some scraggly pines. "This is crazy," he said between breaths. "You can't keep it up. Leave me and get help."

She brushed wet ropes of hair back from her face. "If the positions were reversed, would you leave me?"

"No. But that's—"

"Different?" She had to shout to be heard over the howl of the wind and rain.

"Yeah."

"How's it different? Because I'm a woman?"

"This is getting us nowhere. You've got more guts than anyone I know. But we've got to face facts. We've been at this for over an hour, and we've barely covered a half mile!"

"And we'll cover the next half and the next and the—"

"Anybody ever tell you you're one stubborn woman?"

"Yeah. I seem to remember someone saying that to me. Turns out he was right."

For the first time in an hour, he laughed, though it sounded more of a groan. "You win."

"Good. 'Cause I'm a poor loser."

"I'll remember that."

She stood and then reached down to help him up.

She understood what it cost him to accept her help. She had her own share of pride.

He grunted as he got to his feet.

For the next few minutes, they didn't talk. Rebecca was grateful for the lack of light because it prevented Matt from reading the fear in her eyes and because it prevented her from seeing his expression.

If her fear were reflected in his eyes as well, she was afraid she'd give up then and there. She needed every bit of determination, every ounce of courage she could muster to put one foot in front of the other—again and again.

She scanned the dark sky. The rain showed no indication of letting up.

Neither did she.

The rain pummeled them until they could barely see beyond the next step. She concentrated on keeping her footing as the ground grew more slippery by the moment. She couldn't afford to fall; she might not make it back up again. They continued to follow the river until she held up a hand.

"The river narrows somewhere around here," she said, speaking for the first time in an hour. "It's probably our best chance of crossing it."

If she'd been by herself, she might have waited out the storm. Matt's injury, though, made him more susceptible to the biting cold of the wind and rain. She needed to get him to shelter.

He looked at the swollen river. The water churned around the rocks, spilling over the banks in some places. "Are you sure?"

She followed his gaze. "As sure as I can be."

She helped him sit down against a rock where an overhang provided a bit of shelter. "Let me look around, see if there's any place that looks better." She returned a few minutes later, trying not to let her worry show. "Looks like this is it," she said with determined optimism.

Rebecca uncoiled the rope she'd slung over her shoulder. "Here," she said, handing it to him. "Tie it around your waist." When he'd finished, she did the same, linking them together.

Their arms around each other, they eased off the bank and stepped onto the sand which bordered the river. Their feet sank immediately.

The water, normally peaceful and yellow-brown, was now a frothing gray, mesmerizing in its force, lethal in its power.

"C'mon," Rebecca shouted. "It's not going to get any better."

Cold such as she'd never felt before engulfed her as she waded into the river. She gasped as the icy water whipped around her legs. A dip in the river's bottom caused her to lose her footing and stumble. She caught herself before she went completely under.

Drenched all the way to her shoulders, she shivered violently. With Matt leaning heavily on her, she scrambled for her footing and nearly went under again. Only the rope chaining them together saved her. She paused to catch her breath and saw Matt stagger.

"We can't stop," she yelled above the roar of the water.

Already she could feel her feet and legs begin to grow numb. It wouldn't take many minutes in the water before they lost feeling altogether.

Boulders studded the riverbed. The current tossed her against a particularly sharp one. The blow stunned her, nearly causing her to pass out.

Sheer will kept her conscious, that and the fact that Matt's life depended upon her. The knowledge pumped her adrenaline to flashpoint. They would make it, she vowed silently. The alternative was unthinkable.

Fear and determination sent her energy surging. Together, she and Matt slipped and slid their way toward the far bank. The water rose higher until it lapped around her chest. For each step forward, they were pushed back two. The rope gnawed into her waist.

Then she saw it.

The surging water had loosened a boulder headed straight toward them.

She started to shout a warning, but one look at Matt's face told her he'd already seen it. Their movements hampered by the raging current and the rope tying them together, they dodged to one side, barely missing it.

"Whew," she gasped, realizing how close they'd come to disaster. A blow from the rock could have knocked them unconscious—or worse.

At last, they neared the bank.

"We made it," she cried. "We made it."

"Not quite," he said. He pointed to the boulders which stood like sentinels guarding the riverbank.

She didn't need to be any closer to know they were too high and too slick to climb. She could barely keep her footing as it was! There was no way she could climb up and over the rocks.

Somehow she managed to grab hold of a scraggly bush shooting up in the crevice between two boulders. Water buffeted her against the rocks. Again and again, her body took the blows, but she held on.

It was a chance, maybe their only chance.

"We'll make it." She hoped her voice sounded more confident than she felt.

Before she finished speaking, strong hands grasped her around the waist and thrust her forward until she was atop one of the smaller boulders. Even over the bawl of the wind and the roil of the water, she heard the grunt of effort it cost him to boost her up. Where he found that last rush of strength, she didn't know.

She scrambled to an upright position. Her feet found purchase upon the rock, and she turned to help Matt. "What are you doing?" She watched as he started to unfasten the rope from his waist.

He ignored her and struggled with the knot, his efforts hindered by the cold rain and his own numbed fingers.

She knew what was going to happen if he succeeded in freeing himself. "No!"

"It's the only way. I'll be all right."

He was lying. They both knew it. She'd made it out of the river only because he had shoved her onto the rock. There was no one to help him.

No one but her.

"No way!"

She yanked on the rope, deliberately twisting herself away from him so that he couldn't destroy the link between them. They were bound together, and she didn't intend on severing that tie.

"Let it go, Rebecca!" he yelled, yanking at the knot. The words, so faint that she could barely make them out, sounded above the bellow of the wind.

"You're not getting rid of me that easy. Now grab it and hold on."

Muttering something under his breath, he grasped the rope.

Bracing her feet against the boulder, she began to pull. She ignored the pain as the rope bit into her waist; she ignored the burning of the hemp against her palms; she ignored the rain and wind that battered her. She ignored everything but pulling Matt to safety.

The river lapped at the rocks, further hampering her efforts as she slid on the slick face of the boulder.

"Let go!" Matt bellowed over the bellow of the wind. "You're not strong enough."

That served to have her redouble her efforts. She glared at him. She didn't waste her breath answering but continued pulling. The rope bit deeper into her palms.

For every inch gained, they lost two as the river dragged him back into its fury. Blowing rain stung her face while the wind buffeted her back and forth. Exhaustion was turning her arms heavy, her breathing labored. She knew it was taking its toll on Matt, too, as he fought being swept away by the water.

"Let go," he said hoarsely.

She strained to catch his next words.

"It's no use."

"You let go, and I'll come in after you."

He muttered something about women who didn't have the sense of crazed sheep, but he must have believed her, for he kept hold of the rope.

She measured their progress in fractions of an inch. She didn't think about how much farther they had to go. If she did, she feared she'd give up.

The distance separating them grew smaller, imperceptibly at first, then more noticeably. The knowledge that they were winning the battle against the river fueled her strength, and she redoubled her efforts.

Just when it looked as though they'd made it, Matt fell backward, the pull on the rope dragging her over the boulder. She clawed for something—anything—for purchase. At last her fingers found a jagged edge of rock.

She ignored the searing pain as the rock cut into her flesh.

She felt the rope gnaw at her waist as Matt struggled to stand up. She held on and prayed. Too much time had passed, time they couldn't spare. If she didn't move quickly, they'd both be pulled into the river. She forced herself to her feet and started pulling again.

She was panting now, but not with fear, with hope. She pushed herself to pull harder, still harder. She concentrated, focused every bit of energy she possessed on the task.

It could have been minutes . . . or hours . . . before he crawled over the rock. He laid there, panting heavily. She slumped down beside him, her breath coming in ragged gasps that threatened to turn into sobs. She made a conscious effort to slow her breathing. Cold leached the last trace of energy from her.

"Lady . . . you're . . . something . . . else," he said in between breaths.

"Thanks. I think."

"You're incredible."

She was still cold, but she didn't care. The warmth in his voice was enough to heat her through and through.

The temptation to melt into the embrace was irresistible, and, for a moment, only a moment, she gave in to the luxury of leaning against him, relying on his strength.

She wanted to give way to the weariness that hovered only a breath away, but she pushed herself to her feet and offered Matt a hand. Together, they negotiated the slippery surface of the rock and made their way to the riverbank. "We're going to make it."

"Thanks to you. There's a Navajo tradition that if a squaw saves a brave's life, he becomes her slave."

It felt good to laugh. "You made that up."

"Yeah. But it sounds good, doesn't it?"

It was too dark to see his smile, but she could hear it in his voice. She reached for his hand and found her own caught in his strong grip. Only then did she remember the rope that still bound them together. They fumbled with it until at last Rebecca managed to undo the knots.

They spared a few minutes to catch their breath before starting on their way. The struggle in the river had cost them both, and Rebecca knew she couldn't go much farther. A glance at Matt's face, drawn tight with fatigue and pain, confirmed that he was in even worse shape.

Her legs were shaky, the acrid taste of fear still thick in her throat from their ordeal in the river.

The wind slapped at them, all angry nails and claws. They staggered forward, only to be pushed back by its force. Doggedly, they kept going.

She wished she could see her way more clearly. There were only vague impressions of shapes and sizes, ominously dark, ominously large. She nearly tripped over an exposed root. She caught herself before she plunged to the ground, taking Matt with her.

A branch swung back to sting her lips, and the coppery taste of blood coated her mouth. She swiped at her mouth with the back of her hand, smearing the blood.

Cold, a furtive enemy, crept through her clothes, chilling her right to the bone. If they didn't get warm and dry soon, they were in danger of hypothermia. Even in the summer, hypothermia could prove fatal. At the loss of heat, the body simply shuts down.

Night had fallen like a black curtain, obscuring everything but the cold and wet. She tried not to think beyond putting one foot in front of the other. The ground, slippery from the rain, was as treacherous as the cold. She fought to keep her footing.

"I see it!" she cried. "I see the cabin."

Minutes later, they shoved open the door and stumbled inside. The cabin was dirty, rough, and smelled of stale smoke, and never had anything looked so good in her life.

She settled Matt on the only cot, removed his boot, and checked his leg. The mud had caked over the wound. She dared not try to clean it. All she could do now was pray.

With a start, she realized that her hands were shaking. She hoped Matt hadn't noticed. She supposed that reaction was setting in after their ordeal . . . or was it a response to Matt's nearness?

Right now, she didn't feel like deciding which. The mud she'd smeared on his leg might stop infection. Might—that was the key word.

He tucked a wet strand of hair behind her ear. "Don't worry. I'll be fine."

"I'm not worried," she lied. Even now blood poisoning could be setting in. She'd seen the symptoms of blood poisoning . . . and the effects. Years ago, a boy on the reservation had died when a cut from a rusty can had gone untreated. It started with a slight redness, one that continued to grow.

Before death had claimed him, though, he'd suffered untold agonies as the poison worked its way through his system.

She checked the stove belly. As was the custom, the last person to use the stove had left it set with shredded paper and kindling. She found a box of matches on a shelf above the stove and started a small blaze.

Edging closer, she basked in its warmth and rubbed her arms together. She turned her back to it, feeling like a marshmallow that had been toasted on both sides. Warm at last, she sank onto the cot beside Matt before her legs betrayed her and gave out. She gave a weary sigh as the adrenaline drained out of her.

"Here," he said, handing a blanket to her. "Wrap this around you."

She accepted it gratefully. "Thanks."

The blanket smelled like everything else in the cabin—musty and stale, but it felt wonderful, and she pulled it tighter around her. The coarse material abraded her hands where the rope had cut into them, but she didn't mind. Right now, she was too grateful to be alive.

Before she was too weary to move, she figured she'd better see if she could find something to eat. She rummaged through a rough-hewn cabinet and pulled out a can of peaches. She pried open the lid with a knife she found in a drawer and passed the can to Matt. "Dinner."

She'd winced as her hands had closed around the can. Fortunately, Matt had turned away and hadn't noticed. She fished out a peach half with her fingers and popped it into her mouth.

"Mmm." She sighed in appreciation. "I didn't know canned peaches could taste so good."

They shared the peaches and then drained the can of the syrup. Her stomach grumbled, and Rebecca placed her hand over it, hoping he hadn't heard.

A look at his eyes told her that he had. "There's one more can," he said. "Shall we have it now or save it for later?"

Her stomach rumbled once more, deciding the issue. When they finished eating, they unashamedly licked the juice from their fingers.

"Things could be worse," he said.

"How?"

"We're alive and out of the rain."

She knew he was trying to keep up her spirits, as well as his own. She also knew he was in pain. What she wouldn't give for a bottle of aspirin, anything, to relieve what he must be suffering.

She saw that Matt was rubbing his arms. "You're shivering." She started to pull the blanket away and hand it to him.

"You keep it."

"We'll share."

Their backs braced against the side of the bed, they sat cross-legged in front of the fireplace, the blanket draped around their shoulders.

"You saved my life back there," he said quietly.

"I did what anyone would have done."

"Not anyone. You could've let go, let me take my chances alone. No one would have blamed you."

"I would," she said softly.

He gave a half-turn so that they faced each other. "You're a heroine."

"That's me. A heroine." She laughed at the idea, and he joined in.

It was a reassuring sound after the last harrowing hours.

She watched the play of light and shadow as firelight spilled over his face. His hair, rain-dampened and darkened to the color of wet sand, fell across his forehead. She reached up to push it back.

He caught her hand and drew her to him, then tucked her against him so that her head rested on his shoulder. "Thank you," he said, his voice hoarse. "I'll never forget what you did."

He raised his hand to drag the pad of his thumb

across her lips. His fingers curved around her chin while his thumb continued to trace her mouth.

"You shoved me up the rock. If you hadn't—" She shuddered, knowing she couldn't have made it on her own.

"Let's call it even," he said.

"Even," she murmured.

He turned to her, a crooked grin nipping at his lips. He was so attractive when he forgot to be wary around her.

The snapping and sputtering of the fire, the rain's staccato beat on the roof merged in a comforting rhythm. The warmth of Matt's arms invited her to snuggle deeper. She fought the drowsiness that wrapped itself around her, beckoning to her to give in to it.

Her body clamored for sleep, but she knew she couldn't afford the luxury. She had to watch the fire; even more, she had to check the river. If it rose anymore, they'd have to leave the cabin.

Right now, she wasn't sure if she had the strength to stand, much less leave the warmth of the cabin and hike to higher ground. Her body felt battered and bruised.

She'd close her eyes for a moment . . . only a moment . . .

Matt noticed the fine tremors that shivered along the folds of her shirt, listened as her breathing slowed. Her lashes formed crescent-shaped shadows across her cheekbones. He watched as she gave in to the sleep she so badly needed.

With her lips parted, she looked soft and vulnerable in sleep. She had the kind of beauty to which no man could be immune. Added to that were courage and guts.

Despite her calm determination, Rebecca had been frightened in the river. That, to him, made her actions even more heroic.

Courage wasn't foolhardy bravery. Courage was acknowledging fear and doing what needed to be done in spite of it. Rebecca had courage to spare.

Thunder rumbled while rain continued to pepper the roof. He pushed himself up and grimaced as his leg threatened to give way. There was no sense in them both spending a night on the hard floor.

Slipping an arm under her knees and the other around her shoulders, he picked her up. Her hair spilled over his arm like wet silk. He laid her on the cot and smoothed the blanket over her.

He touched his lips to her hair, then prepared to wait out the night. His ankle ached with a dull throb. He reminded himself it could have been worse—much worse—if Rebecca hadn't treated it as she had. How had she known to put mud on it?

It occurred to him that she had cared for him as a she-wolf cared for its mate. He'd witnessed a wolf refuse to leave a wounded mate, even when its own life was in danger. Wolves, unlike some humans, he reflected with a wry twist of his lips, mated for life.

He hobbled over to the window and peered out.

Seconds later, he heaved a sigh of relief. There was no sign of the river flooding its banks.

He resumed his position in front of the fire, but it wasn't the crackling flames that warmed him. He thought of the meager meal of canned peaches he and Rebecca had shared. He couldn't remember a time when peaches had tasted so good, nor companionship had seemed warmer.

Memories from the past merged with those of the last few hours, swirling around in his brain and creating a soupy perception. He fought to keep consciousness.

He concentrated on Rebecca, but the image of his mother kept superimposing itself over Rebecca's face.

They were nothing alike, he reminded himself fiercely. His mother had abandoned her child without a thought. Rebecca had risked her life to save his own.

He'd meant it when he said that no one, including him, would have blamed her for letting go of the rope, but she'd held onto it and pulled him out of the river with nothing more than stubborn courage.

How she'd done it, he'd never know. He outweighed her by at least seventy pounds; the river had fought her every inch of the way, yet she'd refused to give up. She'd hung on with a grim determination that not even the force of the raging water could defeat.

What was it about her that made him want to hold and protect her? At the same time he could appreciate that she was as strong and capable as anyone—man or woman—he'd ever met.

Her strength was only one facet of her, though. She showed a depth of feeling that staggered him. Her patience with the children, the gentle way she placed them on the horses and eased their fears, had touched a forgotten place in his heart.

He was beginning to understand her anger over the loss of her sheep to Santanna. The wolves were robbing Rebecca of her chance to realize her dream.

He pictured her as she'd been perched on the rock, hair whipping around her blood-smeared face, eyes sparkling with anger when he'd ordered her to let go.

His lips twitched as he remembered how she'd threatened to come in after him if he severed the rope that bound them together. He didn't doubt she'd have done exactly that.

She'd been scared. He'd seen it in her eyes, heard it in her voice. Only a fool wouldn't have been frightened given the fix they were in, but she hadn't given in to her fear. She'd fought her way through it, saving both of them.

It wasn't difficult to picture her as a frontier woman, working to help tame the land alongside her man. She'd be a wife, a helpmeet, a partner in every sense of the word. He was as sure as the heartbeat inside his chest that she would never walk away from her husband or her child.

He stared into the fire, his eyes hard now as ghosts from the past surfaced. His mother had been a nervous, spoiled woman with a hard-edged beauty and a taste for the expensive. She had cared for no one but herself, single-minded in her devotion to getting what she wanted, even if it meant sacrificing her husband and son.

To push the memories away, he shifted his gaze to Rebecca. In her, he could find peace from the ghosts that chased him, refuge from the past that refused to let him go.

She stirred restlessly, tossing the blanket off her. Automatically, he tucked it back around her.

He remembered how she'd pried the trap open, using only a stick. If the stick had slipped, if she had faltered only a bit, the trap could have caught her as well. Even though she'd had only the crude mud to use, she had tended his ankle with gentleness, her touch as soft as her voice.

He watched as she turned on her side, fitting her fist under her chin. She looked hardly older than one of the children she brought to the ranch, her face scrubbed clean by the rain. He brushed a strand of hair back from her cheek, his hand lingering there for a moment. Her skin was warm, flushed from the heat of the fire.

He couldn't shake the memory of Rebecca pulling him from the river. It had been years since he'd needed to lean on another human being—for anything. It reminded him too keenly of the way he had clung to his mother when she had announced that she was leaving.

Rationally, he knew that one had nothing to do with the other. However, it wasn't logic which was ruling his thoughts at the moment. Or his feelings.

He put his hand to his cheek, surprised to find it wet. He wasn't accustomed to tears, especially his own, but they fell freely now.

Rebecca had risked her own life for him. He knew she could have gotten herself to safety, but she'd stayed with him. He'd never forget what she'd done or forgive himself for letting her put herself in that kind of danger.

Outside of his grandfather, no one had ever cared that much about him, putting his needs above their own. The knowledge warmed him even as it humbled him. He felt pressure build in his throat and an anvil lower to his chest.

He cared about Rebecca. It didn't make sense trying to deny it any longer. He'd fought his attraction and his growing feelings for her. Only now was he willing to admit that it was a losing battle.

She had found her way past the barriers he'd kept firmly in place for over two decades. She'd done it simply by being herself.

She was beautiful, but it was more than that. She was also funny, smart, and resourceful. She challenged him, making him think and question things. No other woman had ever affected him that way. He had the uneasy feeling no woman ever would again.

He'd come within a breath of telling Rebecca of

those feelings, and that disturbed him almost more than their life-and-death struggle in the river.

He wasn't in love with her, he assured himself. Sure, he cared about her. He respected her. He even liked her, a lot. She was the first woman he had thought about a future with, the first woman who had truly mattered.

But love? He wasn't about to get lured into that trap. He'd known a long time ago that love would never be a part of his life.

For more than two decades, he'd refused to acknowledge the pain his mother had inflicted upon him by her desertion. He'd grown so adept at hiding his feelings that he'd managed to fool everyone, including himself. His heart, not his head, was in control when he responded to Rebecca.

The realization was a sobering one.

Rebecca had penetrated the wall he'd erected around herself. The only question now was what was he going to do about it.

Chapter Eight

Rebecca awoke with a cramp in her neck. She stretched her arms, felt the resulting tingle shoot up from her elbows to her shoulders as nerve endings sparked with life.

Memory returned slowly. The storm . . . Matt's injury . . . the struggle to find shelter. Struggling up on one elbow, she blinked to adjust to the semi-gloom of the cabin. Watery sunlight trickled through the grimy windows, but it was enough to tell her that the rain had stopped.

She was cold. The fire had gone out, and she got up to rekindle it. Her stiff muscles protested at the movement.

Somehow she'd ended up on the cot. Matt must have put her there last night after she'd fallen asleep. She didn't remember anything beyond sitting in front of the fire, nestled at his side.

She looked up to find Matt slumped in the cabin's one chair. She drank in the sight of him, savoring the opportunity to study him unobserved.

His shirt was untucked, the tails hanging over his jeans and peeking out from under his quilted vest. Dark smudges circled his eyes. Weariness etched itself in every line of his face, and he had never looked more dear.

Her body was bruised and sore, her hands raw and bleeding, but she'd have gone through it all again for this one moment.

She pushed away the blanket that covered her and winced as her hands closed upon the coarse material. A glance at her palms had her quickly looking away.

She pushed herself up. The sound roused him. "Hi," she greeted. "I see you've decided to join the living."

The concern in her eyes belied her teasing words, and she summoned a smile in an attempt to reassure him. In truth, he looked awful.

"Are you all right?" His voice was sandpaper rough.

She was stiff, sore, and longed for a hot bath, but she was alive. "I've been better. What about you?"

Pain had deepened the fine lines that fanned outward from his eyes and furrowed grooves around his mouth. "I'll live."

She raised her eyebrows at the brusqueness of his voice.

"I need to check your leg." She knelt in front of him. Much of the mud had fallen away.

He was so close that she could feel his warm breath upon her cheek. Stubble darkened his jaw, and she wondered what it would feel like if she reached out and touched it.

He shoved her hands away in a brusque motion. "I said that I'll live." It was the tone more than the words that had her brow lifting.

She bit back sharp words when understanding hit her. He was angry, but not with her. He was angry with himself. For a man like Matt, responsibility would always come first.

"Sorry." The single word hardly constituted an apology, but she accepted it, knowing it hadn't come easily.

She nodded.

His expression was troubled. He had more to say; she could feel the words churning just below the surface. She moved closer, as if she could will the truth from him.

Whatever was on his mind didn't make it to his lips, though. His face had become unreadable, as if he had erected a wall between them.

She lifted her hand to his face, then dropped it at the sound of riders. She tried not to resent the interruption. Matt had made it clear that he wouldn't be sharing anything else with her, at least not now.

She rubbed an already filthy sleeve against the window. "It's Ben and some men from the ranch." She flung open the door. "About time you got here."

Ben looked from Rebecca to Matt. "When Maggie and Trapper came home without you, I figured they'd gotten spooked in the storm."

"Are they all right?" Matt asked.

"Not a scratch on them," Ben said. "I rubbed them down myself. They spent the night in a nice, dry barn. We had to wait until daylight before setting out. Are you two all right?"

Rebecca filled him in. "Matt got his leg caught in a trap. I got it open before it broke the bone, but he's in a lot of pain."

Matt gave an impatient grunt. "Rebecca pulled me out of the trap, then the river. She saved my life."

"We saved each other." She lifted her head to smile at him, but the bleak expression in his eyes caused her to draw back.

Matt had withdrawn from her as effectively as if he'd built a wall between them. He turned his attention to Ben. "How'd you know where to find us?"

Ben grinned. "This is the only shelter for miles. I figured Rebecca would head here." He handed a paper sack to Rebecca. "Thought you two might be hungry."

She opened the bag. Inside she found biscuits sandwiched with thick slabs of cheese and ham. She and Matt devoured the food, not bothering to talk until they'd put away two sandwiches apiece and washed them down with a thermos of coffee.

"You're a lifesaver," she said to Ben when she finished.

"I'll remind you of that later," he said. "Right now, let's get this guy to the hospital." He helped Matt mount a brown gelding. "We'll get you to the hospital," he promised. "It just may not be soon. The rain's washed out a lot of roads."

It wasn't the first time the roads had been washed away by a flash flood, leaving them unpassable by anything other than horseback.

The ride home was long and slow as they took several detours to avoid washed out trails and flooded areas. The landscape had changed overnight under nature's caprice. Flowers burned brightly under the sun against newly carved ridges in the ground.

Ben pulled up alongside her. "I was plenty worried when your horses returned without you."

"I'm just glad you found us."

As the journey stretched into an hour, she struggled to keep hold of the reins with her injured hands. They'd started bleeding again, and no amount of blotting them with the sleeve of her shirt would staunch it.

They reached a particularly rough piece of ground, and the motion of the horse's pace became a jarring bounce. Automatically, her hands tightened on the reins.

Once they reached town, they took Matt to the county hospital. "You were lucky," the doctor said after examining his leg and giving him a shot of antibiotics.

Matt thought how much worse it could have been, would have been, if not for Rebecca. "I know."

"You could have lost that leg."

Matt only nodded.

"How did you know to treat it with mud?"

"I didn't," he admitted. "Rebecca deserves the credit."

"Native Americans have used mud for years. Then it caught on in the fancy spas as a skin treatment. But it can also stop infection. Rebecca saved you a lot of pain and, possibly, your leg."

"Where is she?"

"In the next room. She's having her hands looked at."

"Her hands?"

The doctor looked at him in surprise. "Didn't you know? She ripped up her hands pretty bad. She'll be fine, though."

Her hands. It didn't take much figuring to know what had caused the damage.

Rope burns.

Rope burns she'd sustained while saving his life. He'd been too busy trying to hang on to the rope to remember what hemp could do to unprotected skin.

He rejected the doctor's suggestion that he remain at the hospital overnight. He needed to see Rebecca.

She was waiting for him when the hospital released him.

"The doctor said it's all right for you to check out?" She tried to make it a casual question. Was there too much concern in her voice?

"He's leaving it up to me."

He caught her staring at him, and when their eyes

met, she held his gaze. She didn't care if he saw the concern. In fact, she *wanted* him to see it.

"Rebecca, let me look at your hands. Please," he added when she hesitated.

Reluctantly, she held out her hands.

Matt turned them over gently. He flinched at the scrapes and abrasions. "These must hurt like—"

"They hardly hurt at all. Really," she lied when she saw that he didn't believe her. "They look worse than they are."

He fitted a finger under her chin. "You're a rotten liar. I'll bet your waist hurts even more."

Her eyes gave her away. "Some."

Gently he brought her hand to his lips, then pressed a kiss to each of her fingertips. "Why didn't you tell me?"

"What was I supposed to do about it? Whine and cry that they hurt? What good would that have done?"

"You'd never whine."

The simple words warmed her more than could any effusive praise or flattery. The heat of a flush burned across her cheekbones.

She didn't question why a few words from Matt meant so much. She was very much afraid that she already knew the answer.

"Why didn't you tell me how bad they were? If it hadn't been for you . . ." His voice broke, a ragged whisper that tore at her heart.

The concern in his voice thrilled her even as she

warned herself not to read anything more into it than what it was.

His face was gray, bleached to almost white in the dim light of the room. Anger tightened the lines around his mouth.

She knew the target of that anger. Himself. Matt was a man to take on the blame even when it was no fault of his own. A man like Matt wouldn't easily accept that someone had been hurt while saving his life.

"There were more important things to worry about." She saw the self-disgust in his eyes. "I'll be all right."

"I should have been the one taking care of you. Not the other way around."

"You saved my life when you pushed me up those rocks." She reached up and kissed him, a soft brush of lips. When he failed to respond, she drew in an annoyed breath. "I thought we'd settled this," she said, barely able to hide her exasperation.

Pride was at the root of his feelings.

His lips flattened in a tight line. "That was before—"

"Before what?"

"Before I saw what you'd done to yourself."

"If you'd stop being so selfish, you'd see that I'm right."

"Selfish?"

"Believing that you can control everything that happens to people is a kind of selfishness."

"I don't—"

"Don't you?"

That stopped him. "Okay. So maybe I like to be in control."

She raised a brow. "Just maybe?"

A half smile lifted the corners of his mouth.

"Stop blaming yourself. These scratches will fade a lot faster than the guilt you insist on heaping upon yourself."

Matt thought it over. Rebecca couldn't be right. He wasn't so egocentric as to believe he had to be in control of everything and everyone, was he? Only a fool thought he could control the world.

He'd been vulnerable last night, shaken by what had happened, by what had almost happened.

"It wasn't your fault," she said.

"You should have told me."

Rebecca's gaze remained steady on his. "I did what was needed. No more. No less. Let it go."

He wished he could. He wished he could forget that she'd risked her life to save his because that might allow them to go back to the easy friendship they'd enjoyed. He wished for all that and more.

He wanted to reach out and snare a strand of her hair, urging her toward him, but he kept his hands to himself, knowing if he touched her, he wouldn't be able to let her go.

There was nothing in her gold eyes but honesty, and Matt felt something lurch inside him. He'd never before thanked anyone for saving his life, and he'd made a mess of it.

He gave a short nod which, they both knew, didn't signify agreement.

It happened sooner than she'd anticipated.

By the time they returned to the ranch, Matt had pulled away from her. He'd become cool, polite, and reserved. She'd expected it, but she couldn't stifle the ache that settled in her heart.

Even after all they'd been through together, he'd pulled back into himself with no hint remaining of the man who'd opened up to her, sharing his dreams, his fears.

She realized in a rush of self-honesty that she wanted more from Matt than friendship. She wanted it all, and she'd never be happy with less. She placed a hand on his shoulder and felt a shudder go through him.

"Thank you," he said, the stiff formality in his voice adding a fresh layer to her disappointment. "For everything." The closed expression in his eyes smarted far more than the abrasions on her hands.

She felt his withdrawal as surely as she would if he'd taken a step back from her.

It was deliberate. Perhaps that was what hurt the most, the realization that he knew what he was doing and felt compelled to do it anyhow.

She shouldn't care, but it was too late for that. Far too late. She wanted to rail at him for his decision to hurt both of them. Then she saw the pain that shadowed his eyes.

If what they'd shared on the trail didn't count for something, oh, not a commitment or anything like that, not yet, then she had to wonder what they did have. She'd believed they had a friendship, an honest acceptance of each other. Now she wondered.

"You're not easy," she said, giving voice to her thoughts. "You only let me go so far before you start backing away."

"There are reasons—"

"I know. I guess it's up to me to change your mind." She threw the words down as a challenge and prayed he'd take her up on them.

Matt flattened his hands on his hips, his stance clearly saying No Trespassing.

The time for sharing was past.

She invited Matt to stay at the house while he recuperated. His refusal came as no surprise, but she couldn't help a sigh of disappointment.

She longed to repeat the kiss they had shared on the trail. She took a step in his direction, and, for a moment, forgot Ben and Uncle Ray were there, forgot everything but Matt.

Uncle Ray's voice brought her back to reality. "Ben will drive you to your home," her uncle said to Matt. "You must stay off that leg."

"Thanks," Matt said, his eyes on Rebecca. "For everything."

Uncle Ray spoke little after Matt's departure. He didn't seem to expect her to add much, for which she was grateful. Her thoughts kept returning to Matt and how he'd shut her out.

"You are thinking about him," her uncle said. His smile was gentle and knowing. "He is a good man."

"I know."

"Do not let him push you away."

"Why does he do it?" All of her hurt poured into the words.

"Self-preservation." Uncle Ray patted her hand. "He has been hurt in the past. Be patient with him."

She didn't bother to ask how her uncle knew of Matt's past. Uncle Ray had a way of knowing things about people.

"I'd never hurt him. I love him."

Uncle Ray nodded. "I have seen how you look at him. You wear your heart in your eyes. There are loves which will take you from sunrise to sunset. And there is the one love which will take you from sunrise to sunrise and all the sunrises after that. Guard it carefully for it is priceless above all else."

She felt a curious tingling in her chest. So this was what love felt like. If it were so good, then why was she so scared?

The time was coming when she wouldn't be able to

keep her feelings from Matt. Until then, she was content to hold them close to her heart.

Two hours later, Rebecca looked at the account book and bills littering her desk and wondered when she'd become a paper pusher instead of a rancher. If she could swing it financially, she'd hire an accountant and let him handle the ever increasing paperwork.

Right now, she was putting every cent she could back into the ranch but maybe next year. She turned back to the pile of bills, but, again, her attention wandered.

She switched off her computer and pushed her chair back from the desk. Crossing the room, she looked out the window, trying to focus on the dazzling light the sun cast on the tin roof of the work shed. It, too, failed to hold her attention.

She rationalized her inability to concentrate with the thought of her injured hands. They had begun to throb, but she knew it was more than the pain that kept intruding on her work. It was something much more elemental and far more disturbing . . . the memory of Matt's withdrawal from her.

She wouldn't let him slip behind the shadow of his past. He deserved a chance at happiness. *They* deserved a chance.

If he'd give voice to his feelings for her, they could move forward. She knew he cared for her. She even dared hope that caring had grown into love, but he'd never used the word.

Maybe she could teach him that feelings didn't have

to be feared. Matt had so much to give . . . if only she could convince him of it.

In the meantime, they still had the matter of the wolves to settle between them.

Gravel and dust spat from beneath the tires as Rebecca pulled out of the town hall parking lot two nights later. She'd endured a three hour meeting.

She'd come down hard on one of her neighbor's ideas to place a bounty on the wolves. Santanna and his pack had raided another ranch the night before. Sentiment was running high against the animals.

She could imagine the pain in Matt's eyes if he learned of it. But what was she to do? She couldn't turn her back on her neighbors, but neither could she stomach the idea of a wolf hunt. Every fiber revolted at the idea.

She couldn't watch while the wolves were systematically destroyed without trying to stop it. Whatever losses she'd suffered because of them couldn't justify a whole-scale slaughter. She'd been deceiving herself if she'd ever thought she could go along with such a thing.

Word had gotten out how Matt had been injured by one of the traps. Murmurs of sympathy had gone through the room, but underneath there had been something darker. She'd heard more than a few comments that maybe he'd gotten what he deserved.

"The wolf-lover got himself caught like any other

varmint, huh? I call that justice." That had come from Rudy.

Rudy had probably set the traps himself, she thought. The traps were illegal, but the local law turned a blind eye to them. Now the other ranchers were talking about putting a bounty on the animals. There had to be another way. There had to be.

She wanted answers for her town. She wanted answers for Matt and the wolves. She wanted answers for herself.

At home three hours later, she pushed back her chair, smiling. She didn't have all the details figured out yet, but she was convinced her plan would work. Once she worked out the snags, she'd take it to the other ranchers. She'd make them see reason.

It was so simple that she wondered why she hadn't thought of it before. The canyon where she'd taken Matt, virtually unusable because of its isolation, occupied the southernmost tip of her property.

Her lips quirked as she recalled the story of how her great-grandfather had won it in a horse race years ago. Bordered by a ridge, it was sheltered from the worst of the elements and fed by an underground spring—a perfect home for the wolves.

She did some quick calculations. It might work. A half-smile erased the tired lines that had scored her forehead a short while ago.

Her excitement grew by the moment. Moving the

wolves to the canyon where they couldn't threaten stock should satisfy the ranchers.

Matt would still want to tag the animals, but she could help with that. Her pulse quickened at the thought that they'd be working together. It would give them a chance to work toward a goal rather than against each other.

She smiled and thought how comfortable she was with him.

Her smile faded. Once Matt's job was finished, he'd probably be reassigned. It was a troubling thought, all the more so because she'd only just realized how lonely her life had been before she met him, how lonely it would be again when he left.

If only he could admit that he loved her, then maybe . . .

That feeling remained with her through the weekend when Matt arrived to help with the art program.

"He shows compassion," Uncle Ray said with a nod in Matt's direction as he helped the kids from the reservation.

"He cares about the kids. And the wolves." *And maybe*, she thought, *he cared about her as well*.

Was that why he had been so careful that they didn't spend time alone together?

Since they had returned from the hospital, Matt had made sure that Uncle Ray or Ben or the children from the reservation were always with them. She knew he was finding excuses to keep from being alone with her.

Matt had taken to spending Saturday afternoons at the ranch, helping Rebecca with her art classes. Right now he was encouraging Sarah to draw Maggie as she stood in the corral.

"You said I could go for a ride," Sarah reminded him at the end of the lesson.

"You're right."

Matt lifted the child from her wheelchair and placed her on Maggie. Following Rebecca's instructions, he fastened the straps which held her legs to the saddle.

He led Maggie around the corral.

Judging that she'd had enough after twenty minutes, he undid the straps that kept Sarah legs in place and then carefully lifted her down and carried her to where one of the ranch hands waited with her wheelchair.

"You're doing great," he said.

Matt looked forward to his time with the children. The time had quickly stretched from a couple of hours to half a day, then a whole day.

Once again, he reminded himself that he and Rebecca were friends, but he was starting to depend on her too much.

He needed time. Time to step back, put some distance between himself and Rebecca. He'd allowed things to move too quickly, too intensely. That would have to change. It was time to inject some logic into the situation.

He didn't intend to trade his independence for the

heartache of marriage. Hadn't his parents taught him anything?

By the following day, he was no closer to resolving his feelings about Rebecca. It didn't help that they planned to spend the day together transporting the wolves to the canyon.

He worked to keep their relationship at a casual level as they tagged the wolves in preparation for moving them.

Rebecca was a tireless worker, patient with the animals, savvy enough to keep her wits about her when they turned skittish.

He'd felt her turn a puzzled gaze on him several times during the day. Obviously his decision to downplay whatever was between them bothered her. He regretted that, but it couldn't be helped.

"That's the last of them," he said.

When they were finished, they took the animals to the canyon. There, with the natural shelter provided by the ridge rimming the area, the animals would be safe. What's more, they'd no longer be a threat to the ranchers.

When Rebecca had explained about the empty canyon, he'd asked who owned the land. She had brushed aside his question and reminded him of the work still ahead of them. He'd dropped the subject, but not his interest. A trip to the records room at the town hall several days ago confirmed what he'd already suspected—the land belonged to Rebecca.

He hadn't been surprised. He'd already known that she cared more about the wolves than she admitted, but to give up part of her land as a refuge for the wild animals spoke more eloquently than words of her concern.

He smiled, thinking she'd never be one for pretty words and speeches. She was a woman who did what had to be done without drawing attention to it. It was one of the things that had first drawn him to her.

Without his volition, thoughts of how Rebecca's hands and waist must have felt on fire as she pulled him to safety swam through his mind. He remembered how she'd kept her hands hidden from him, obviously wanting to keep him from knowing about the pain she'd endured while saving his life.

He knew that he shouldn't have the feelings for her that he harbored. He knew, also, that self-preservation demanded that he not give a name to those feelings.

They worked well together. In the space of only a couple of weeks they'd found each other's rhythms, understood their likes and dislikes. Tagging the last of the wolves and transporting them to the canyon had been a fitting end to the day.

They stood there now, arms linked, more in harmony than he'd have believed possible a month ago.

Straggly trees provided shade. Summer-dried grass, dotted with a few hardy wildflowers, carpeted the area. Jack rabbits and other small game would provide a steady supply of food for the wolves. A jagged ridge of rocks, a natural fenceline, bordered it and would ensure that the wolves remained within the canyon. Caves, carved from the rock centuries ago, provided shelter.

Forgetting his earlier decision to keep his distance, Matt picked her up and swung her around. "It's great," he said. "Thanks to you."

"It was a joint effort. You and me. We make a pretty good team, don't we?"

Her rich voice wrapped itself around him until it reached down inside his heart. Her words drew him into a warm, fresh sea and drowned him there in a sweetness he'd never known. He struggled to surface, to pull out of the snare of love he read in her gaze.

Slowly he set her down, but he couldn't make himself let go of her completely and, instead, framed her face with his hands. "The best."

Joy suffused her face, and he felt something inside him turn over with an unfamiliar, painful tumble.

Chapter Nine

*T*he best.

Rebecca's heart swelled at Matt's words. She didn't wait for his kiss. She took matters into her own hands and pressed her lips to his.

With her lips centered on his, she was grounded. She needed no other support. Still, her hands moved to his shoulders, then around his neck. So close were they that she couldn't tell where her heartbeat stopped and his started, and she knew with absolute certainty this was what she'd been waiting for all of her life.

Her breath caught somewhere between her lungs and her throat. She struggled to release it. She wished that her heart didn't pound like a sledgehammer in her chest and waited for her insides to settle.

He drew in a shuddering breath, as if he, too, had been shaken to the core.

She'd always hoped that someday she would meet a man who would stir her in a way too powerful to resist, too important to ignore.

She loved him.

Did he have any idea of what kind of effect he had on her? She decided to take the risk, to share what was in her heart. She took a step back, needing to see in his face what was in her heart.

"I love you." She'd done it. There was no going back.

He took her into his arms.

Her heart was doing somersaults, sweet tumbles of joy as she realized all she'd ever wanted was hers. She steadied herself against him.

"I'm not what you need," he said.

She put a finger to his lips. "You're everything I'll ever need, everything I'll ever want." Love, hot and sweet, welled up inside her. Emboldened by her own feelings, she repeated the three most important words she would ever say. "I love you."

A great stillness settled over them, as if a photographer had snapped a picture, forever freezing the moment into a single frame.

The spell snapped when he pulled back, ever so slightly. She felt, more than heard, the sharp intake of breath.

She lifted her head. "I love you." She waited. Hoping. Praying.

She could still smell the male scent that was his alone. She inhaled deeply and knew that it would be forever imprinted in her memory.

His eyes were shadowed. "I care about you. You know that."

What was he saying? Her smile trembled around the edges, but she managed to keep it in place.

"I care about you more than I ever thought possible."

She heard the hitch in his breath, the husky note in his voice that told her everything she wanted to know. She'd never heard him use those tones until now.

Not even when he'd nearly lost his leg in the vicious trap, when he'd cried out his pain in harsh, urgent syllables had his voice broken with emotion as it did now. She'd started to believe that he couldn't, or wouldn't, allow himself to bare his feelings.

Silently, she rejoiced that she'd been wrong. "You love me." She laced her arms around his neck. "You love me."

Gently, he freed himself. "I care about you."

Moved by the rough feeling in his voice, she nodded. "I know."

Something in the way he was looking at her caused a wad of fear to stick in her throat. A jerk of panic beneath her skin told her that she wasn't going to like what he was about to say.

"I'm trying to be totally honest with you. I'd do anything for you. Anything but—"

Her smile dissolved altogether, then turned upside

down as she realized what he was trying to say. "Anything but say you love me. Is that it?" She willed him to deny the words. To laugh away her fears. To take her in his arms and tell her that he loved her as much as she loved him.

She shivered. It wasn't the sudden chill of the wind, though, that had goosebumps puckering her flesh.

He gripped her shoulders. "I can't be what you want."

She shook off his hands. "You already are."

"That's where you're wrong." He shoved a hand through his hair.

She swallowed tightly, trying to ease the dryness in her throat and the aching disappointment. "You know what's ironic? You already love me. I see it in your face. I feel it when you touch me. But you can't say the words. You can't force yourself to say them because if you did, you'd be vulnerable like the rest of us. And that's the one thing you won't allow yourself to be.

"I won't walk out on you." She saw the trace of understanding in his eyes. "I won't let you down." She paused, letting her words sink in. "And I won't leave you."

"How can I be sure?" he asked, so softly she almost missed it.

"Because I love you."

He wanted to return the words. She saw it in the slight parting of his lips, in the darkening of his eyes.

"Rebecca." His voice was gentle, but she could hear the underlying pain.

If he didn't know what there was between them, she couldn't tell him.

His eyes wore the shuttered look she'd noticed when she first met him, the look they assumed whenever he was afraid of showing what he felt. She'd have to live with the knowledge that she'd done that.

"I care about you," he said once more, his voice tinged with desperation. "Can't that be enough?"

His words were paltry crumbs, and they both knew it.

He gathered her to him, his arms closing around her. His mouth sought hers in a gentle kiss.

It was so simple, when they were like this.

With a soft murmur of regret, he set her away from him. She watched as the hand against his thigh balled into a fist.

She felt the loss of his arms around her. Even more, she felt his emotional withdrawal. A coldness washed over her until she was numb from it.

"I'm sorry," he whispered. "I wish things were different."

She closed her eyes against the tenderness in his voice. Somehow that made it worse, since they both knew that it wasn't things that needed to be different. It was him.

"Go. Run away," she said.

"That's not fair."

"Maybe not. But it's true. You're running away from love. A word you can't even say. You'd rather waste the present on the past."

He loved her. She knew it. In time, she could teach him that love could heal the pain he was carrying inside. She had love enough to wait while he accepted his own feelings.

Could she wait? Slowly, she shook her head in answer to her silent question. Unless Matt could accept that she loved him, unless he could allow himself to be vulnerable by admitting his own love, they didn't have a future, and she loved him too much to accept half a life with him.

Tears burned in her eyes, but she refused to wipe them away. She wasn't ashamed of them. A breaking heart deserved a few tears. Briefly she wondered whether it was possible to die from a shattered heart. The way she was feeling right now, she wasn't going to bet against it.

She saw the denial in his eyes. *Even now he was lying to himself*, she thought. "When you decide to stop living in the past and step into the present, you know where I'll be.

"I love you. I always will. Nothing's going to change that. Not even you." Her voice shook with the words.

"If I didn't know better, I'd almost believe in happy endings," he said. The smile he gave her was infinitely sad, a slight tug at the corner of his lips. "You don't need me. You're going to be just fine on your own, Rebecca Whitefeather." He grazed his knuckles across the angle of her cheekbone.

"I know that. But will you?" She didn't give him a

chance to answer but reached up to kiss him once more. "Good-bye, Matt. You'll wonder. You'll wonder what could have been if you'd had the courage to take a chance on love. On us."

He lifted a hand as if to press his palm against her arm. She saw the hesitation in his eyes, then his fingers slowly curled, and he lowered his arm. A momentary hope flared to life, only to wither away once more.

She climbed astride Maggie, then touched her heels to the mare's flanks. She clung to the reins and resisted the urge to look back. If she did, she wasn't sure she'd have the strength to leave.

Her emotions raw, she rode away—from Matt, from the life they could have together, not sure if she ached more for him or for herself.

Matt imagined he could still hear the echo of Rebecca's words of condemnation in the still air of the afternoon.

He didn't know why he continued to stare in the direction she'd taken except that it had something to do with the empty feeling that gnawed at the pit of his stomach.

He wanted to go after her, but if he gave into that need, he might say what he didn't mean, what he didn't believe in, what he wasn't ready for, would never be ready for. For the span of a heartbeat, his resolve threatened to crumble as he recalled the pain in her eyes.

It didn't surprise him that Rebecca would tell him of

her feelings for him. Another woman would have played coy, keeping those feelings to herself until she'd obtained a similar declaration from him.

Not Rebecca. Her honesty, her total lack of pretense, had gutted him.

If he had learned anything about Rebecca Whitefeather, it was that she was utterly fearless in confronting whatever obstacle stood in her way, even when that obstacle was him.

Words to call her back hovered on his lips. He'd say what she longed to hear, and everything would be all right. They could make a life together, a good life. Though he didn't love her, he did care for her. Marriages had been built on less. Even as the thought formed, he knew he couldn't do it.

He hardened his heart. He'd done the right thing, the only thing, for both himself and Rebecca.

I love you. I always will. Nothing's going to change that. Not even you. The words slid through his mind with the ease of a knife, cutting through defenses he didn't know he had.

She had been wrong. He wasn't running away. He'd never run from anything in his life.

He tried to push her image from his mind but discovered he couldn't do it. She'd looked so lovely, the sun slanting shafts of light against her hair.

Rebecca had said that she loved him. She wouldn't exaggerate, he knew. It wasn't her style. Simple words said with simple truth.

He shaded his eyes against the harsh rays of the sun. Deliberately, he turned his back on the meadow where the wolves cavorted like playful children. It was too painful, a reminder of Rebecca.

She had asked for the one thing he couldn't give.

Love.

Automatically, Matt folded the clothes and packed his belongings. His job was done. He wouldn't be coming back. His lips quirked humorously as he remembered the vow he'd made to himself that he was here to stay, but that was before he'd met Rebecca. Before she'd told him that she loved him. Before he'd made it clear that he didn't want that love.

He'd already made arrangements to lease the land. A neighbor offered to take Trapper until Matt decided what to do with him. Later, when he could think straight, he'd decide what to do with the house.

He imagined he could still smell the sweet fragrance of her, wrapping its spell around him.

It had been hard, so much more difficult than he thought it would be, to walk away from her. How could he have known that it would rip the heart from him to see her devastated face?

He promised himself one last ride. With that in mind, he headed to the barn and saddled Trapper.

The big gelding whinnied softly.

Matt took his time, wanting to memorize every feature of the land, to understand its pull for him even as he was leaving it.

He would miss the beautiful, if stark, surroundings. The land would continue on as it had, surviving the vagaries of nature and man's attempt to civilize it. He let his gaze stray to the mountains that seemed suspended from the sky as wispy clouds cut them in half.

With one last look at the prairie, Matt turned. He had one more errand to take care of before he left. After making sure that Rebecca was nowhere around the corral or barn, he found Uncle Ray repairing harnesses.

Matt started to say good-bye when Ray stopped him.

"You will visit the sweat lodge. Then we will talk."

Matt didn't think to argue but only nodded.

The sweat lodge, on the outskirts of the reservation, was a roughly built shelter of poles and animal skins, the roof made of branches woven together.

Matt was given a blanket and told to leave his clothes outside. After shedding his clothes, he stepped inside.

The heat nearly knocked him over. He braced himself, letting his eyes adjust to the dimness. Coals burned in one corner, damp cloths tented over them to produce steam.

"Come," Ray said. "You will find that which you are seeking if your heart is open."

Was it, Matt wondered? Was his heart open? How did he know?

"Is that a promise?" He regretted the sarcastic words as soon as they were out of his mouth.

Ray seemed not to have noticed, though.

Matt sat down on a crudely-made bench and waited. For what, he wondered.

He watched the others. With the exception of himself and a young boy whom Ray told him was going through a tribal rite of passage, the men, all members of the reservation community, appeared over seventy.

"When do I start getting all this wisdom?" Matt asked.

Ray's voice was gently chiding. "You must wait. Listen. Watch."

"You told me I'd find answers here."

"You are impatient. The spirits will not be rushed. They will work in their own time, in their own way. You must first empty your mind of all that troubles it."

Matt settled back on the bench, willing his body to relax, to adapt to the heat.

"Do not fight it," Ray cautioned. "Let the heat into you. It will become one with you. Only then can your mind see beyond the mist."

Seconds bled into minutes, minutes into hours. Aside from the few instructions Ray whispered to Matt, talking was discouraged. The men spoke in low tones and then only when necessary.

Matt wet his lips, finding even that small gesture exhausting. Just when he was sure he could stand it no longer, he felt the tension inside him start to melt away. It flowed out of him, leaving his body limp, but his mind at peace. Was this what Uncle Ray had referred to?

Images of Rebecca, images that he'd tried to banish,

rolled through his mind. He couldn't forget those moments when he'd felt that she could not only read him but knew him better than anyone else ever had.

He wanted to believe that she truly loved him. He wanted it more than he could remember wanting anything, but life had taught him hard lessons, ones he wasn't likely to forget.

He'd get over her . . . eventually. A humorless smile tightened his lips.

At the end of the eight hours, he staggered out of the sweat lodge. His muscles tingled with the after-effects of the heat. He was no nearer to finding the answer he sought than he had been before, though.

"The spirits do not always answer as we expect," Ray said, apparently sensing Matt's disillusionment. "The answer must come from inside you." He patted Matt's shoulder. "The sweat lodge is only a place where the spirits can talk to you. It is up to you to listen."

Matt could only watch in amazement. Ray, at seventy-something, had spent the same eight hours in the sweat lodge that Matt had, yet he moved with the springy step and the squared shoulders of a young man. Matt estimated that it would be another hour before he could move again. If that.

Ray pressed a steaming cup into Matt's hands. "Drink."

Matt eyed the dark brew warily. "What's in it?"

"Tea. Corn silk and chicory. It will restore your body's fluids."

Matt drank deeply, scowling as the bitter concoction slid down his throat. Much as he wanted to believe in the healing powers of the sweat lodge, nothing had changed. He would leave, just as he'd planned.

"You must make peace with your past," Ray said.

Matt regarded the older man with a faint smile. "Someday I hope I'll be half as wise as you."

Hours later, Ray's counsel echoed Matt's thoughts, and he knew that before he could go forward, he had to settle things between himself and his father. Matt could never condone his father's unethical practices, but he could respect the man in other ways and maybe, just maybe, convince Erskin to give up the company's practice of illegal dumping.

By the following morning, Matt was still trying to summon some enthusiasm for the idea of returning to California. Without Rebecca at his side, though, the future stretched bleakly before him. She'd made him feel whole again. She had unsnarled the tangle of hurt and abandonment inside of him, an ache he hadn't even been aware of . . . and she had done it unconsciously, by loving him.

Love.

The word he'd shied away from for so many years. The word that Rebecca had needed him to say. The word he couldn't say.

So what was he left with?

Nothing. He tried reminding himself that that's what he'd had before Rebecca found her way into his life, but the emptiness he experienced now was that much more painful because he knew what fulfillment felt like.

It was a healing kind of love, and he'd thrown it back in her face. He wasn't the man for her. He didn't know *how* to love a woman, least of all a woman like Rebecca, who deserved everything good in life. He set his jaw against the curl of regret that settled inside him.

She would find someone else eventually. Someone who could give her everything she deserved. Someone who wasn't scarred by the past. Someone who knew how to love and to be loved.

If he were any kind of a friend, he'd be happy for her when it happened, and he would be, he promised himself fiercely, even if it killed him.

That didn't stop a greasy pit of jealousy from churning in his belly at the idea.

Chapter Ten

Rob Estes was the town veterinarian. He had treated Rebecca's animals for more than seven years. He was a kind man. A good man. So when he asked her out, she accepted.

Matt had been gone for two weeks, and with every day that passed, her hope that he would call or write died a little more.

She tried to enjoy the evening of dinner and a movie, a romantic-comedy that should have lifted her spirits. It didn't. It only served to depress her further.

When Rob leaned forward to kiss her goodnight, she turned her head so that it was her cheek that met his lips.

His eyes registered his disappointment. "I'm sorry. I presumed too much."

"No. I'm the one who's sorry." She said a gentle goodnight and let herself out of the car.

The darkness closed in around her. The air had turned cool, but she didn't go inside. She sniffed and caught the smell of wood smoke. Uncle Ray must have lit a fire.

The night held a much-needed gentleness that had been denied to the day, but it failed to ease the pain that ravaged her spirit.

Other men suffered by comparison to Matt. It was unfair to everyone involved, but there it was. She thrust away the memories before the tears could start again. She'd wasted enough time on them. She'd have a life-time of regrets. She didn't need to dwell on them now.

Hearts do not really break, she decided. They may get bruised or cracked, but they don't break. She was living proof of it. If her heart were broken, she wouldn't be able to feel.

She wouldn't be accepting any more dates. Better to remain alone than to be with someone she didn't love. That was the worst kind of loneliness.

With a tired sigh, she looked up at the night sky, so beautiful and star-filled but so empty of answers. What had she expected?

If she couldn't find the answer on her own, how had she believed she would find it in the heavens? Not even the caress of the soft night air on her face could soothe the sting of loss.

Matt was everything she'd ever wanted. She bowed her head as despair pressed against her heart.

Sleep had eluded her for the last week. If she were lucky, she managed to snatch a few hours near morning when her exhausted mind finally gave up the struggle. Inevitably, she awoke to the depressing memory that nothing had changed.

She tried to remember what it had felt like to be happy. She had the sinking feeling that memories might be all she had to look forward to.

Matt had brought her to life, teaching her the joy possible between a man and a woman, but the lesson had a painful adjunct. She now knew the torment of loneliness, and knew she would have to face the long days when every sound, every breath, reminded her of him.

When she went inside, she found Uncle Ray waiting up for her. She knew her feeble attempt at a smile didn't fool him.

"You disappoint me, niece."

Rebecca could only stare. It stung. It was the harshest thing her uncle had ever said to her. What was there about Uncle Ray's disappointment that weighed heavier than that of others?

"I'm sorry," she said stiffly.

He made a dismissing motion with his hand. "You disappoint yourself."

She couldn't argue with that. She'd moped around the house for two weeks, neglecting the ranch and her responsibilities to it.

Work had been her salvation in the past when pain

threatened to overwhelm her. She thought of the sheep that needed to be moved from one meadow to another, the dozens of chores that needed to be done to keep the ranch going. It shamed her that she'd let her uncle, Ben, and the others take up the slack that her self-absorption had created.

The anger drained from her and, with it, the last of the energy to pretend that her life had not fallen apart when Matt had told her he was leaving.

"I'm sorry," she said again.

Ray placed a strong hand on Rebecca's arm. "When your heart is troubled, you must look outside of yourself for the medicine to cure it."

She understood. She'd been so wrapped up in her own heartache that she had neglected those who needed her. Deliberately she called to mind the blessings in her life. The important things, the things that made her who she was and what she was, were still intact: Uncle Ray, Ben, the kids from the res, the land.

Then why did she feel like a boat whose mooring lines had all been cut? Why did she have such a sense of emptiness?

"I won't let you down again," she promised. "I'll start pulling my weight."

To her surprise, Uncle Ray shook his head. "The work will wait for you. Go to the mountains you love and make your peace. Then return to us."

Rebecca pressed a kiss to the wrinkled cheek. "Thank you, Uncle."

The following morning, she headed to the barn. Maggie greeted her with a whicker of pleasure.

The day beckoned. Such a day deserved to be savored, not endured, which was all she'd been doing the past week. The very air was a balm to her skin, the sun a warm caress. Despite her heartache, she felt her spirits lift a fraction.

Guilt gnawed at her once again for shirking her work, but Uncle Ray had insisted that she spend the day in the mountains. As he had so many times in the past, he had known what she needed before she did herself.

A sparse rain had left the sky overcast, but the early morning sun speared through the clouds long enough to paint the landscape with a pink glow.

The mountains were a place where it seemed time had stopped, civilization but a distant memory. Wild and unfettered by the trappings man had brought to the wilderness, they summoned her.

Rebecca navigated the torturous trail with practiced ease. When she reached a clearing, she tugged at Maggie's reins. The view stretched before her, a panorama of unmatched beauty.

She never came here without feeling transported back in time where her imagination could take flight. That had always been the appeal for her. The scenery, magnificent though it was, was secondary.

Still, she spared a glance for it. Mountains, stripped of their greenery, rose like altars to the sky. Gorges, deep and forbidding, scarred the land. In the distance, the river, her enemy just weeks ago, meandered peacefully through the valley.

The land worked its magic on her as it always did, pulling her into another dimension, teasing her to leave all her troubles behind. She gave herself up to the quiet and let the peace settle over her, absorbing the serenity.

Pink and orange streaked the sky, a vivid contrast to the brown of the scorched earth. With the air still retaining a hint of the night's chill and the heat of the day only a promise, she could believe in dreams.

She stood there, hands braced on her hips, and tried not to think of Matt.

Of course, she thought of him.

She watched two deer, a doe and her fawn, walk quietly out of the forest to drink from the sluggish creek, their delicate legs lost in the low-lying mist that layered the ground. Content, she remained hidden, hoping the deer would not catch her scent. The scene, as peaceful as the lazy clouds that scudded across the sky, soothed her troubled heart.

The vista stretched before her was enough to take her breath away. Mountains poked their peaks through low-slung clouds. The clouds themselves were cotton puffs against the sky. Sunshine filtered through them, dappling the ground in a crazy quilt of shadow and light.

A perfect day for a picnic. Memories rushed back of another such day, a picnic shared with a very special man. Memories were all she had now, and she hoarded them with the stinginess of a miser storing away gold.

She shivered in her thin cotton shirt and hugged her arms to her. Goosebumps puckered her skin, but she scarcely noticed as a sound above snagged her attention.

A raven soared overhead. The bird, beautiful in the way only a wild thing can be, glided through the sky, its wing span easily four or five feet. Pride and strength, she thought, a powerful combination. In a raven. Or a man.

Her lips folded together as she thought about the reason behind Matt's refusal to admit that he loved her.

His mother's desertion had left him a legacy of distrust and fear. Rebecca's heart ached for the lonely little boy who blamed himself for his mother's abandonment and for his father's withdrawal.

How could a child understand a mother's desertion and a father who guarded his feelings, afraid to let anyone close? A nine-year-old child shouldn't have to carry that kind of burden. If only he'd let her close enough, she knew she could teach him that love didn't have to end in pain.

Would she ever get over this longing for him? For a moment, she wished he'd never found his way into her life, never taught her what it meant to love, to be loved.

She rejected the idea immediately. Those weeks with Matt were the most wonderful time of her life, and if she were given the choice, she'd do the same thing over again.

She loved him. She always would.

Somehow, she'd get over it. Somehow, she'd get over him, but in her heart, she knew there'd be scars.

She resolved to put him out of her mind, for at least the rest of the day. For the most part, she succeeded.

Okay, an errant thought might have slipped past her resolve. Stray images of the way his hair slipped over his forehead, of the sudden flashes of humor that touched his eyes, of the warm taste of his lips, might have found their way into her mind.

Her need to see the wolves had her urging her horse faster. She felt the change in the air. Maggie must have sensed the difference, too, for she whickered.

It grew cooler as they climbed until at last they were picking their way over the rocky ridge that rimmed the meadow. Here the land, fed by a small spring, blossomed with color.

Sunlight silvered the wild grass. The air was garden-fresh, peppery with the after-scent of rain. Sunlight peeked through slits in the clouds, bright patches against the darker shadows. The rainwashed air whispered onto her face.

The still damp grass and the earthy aroma of dirt scented the air. Fortunately, this rain had brought a much-needed soaking to the ground rather than the wild storm of a few weeks ago. She could make out the stream, now lazily meandering within its banks, the violence that had nearly cost Matt and herself their lives only a memory.

A shiver traced down her spine as she recalled those few moments where she feared the water would claim both of them. She pushed the frightening pictures away and concentrated on the beauty surrounding her.

A thimble-sized breeze lifted the hair from her forehead. Mist blew against her face, a scrap left over from the rain.

A shrill trumpeting had her standing in the stirrups, straining to see in the distance.

Santanna led his pack, his arrogance not a wit changed by his recent captivity. He stopped, ears pricked, head cocked. Apparently satisfied that nothing threatened him or his pack, he signaled for the others to join him.

Rebecca watched him, moved as always by his proud bearing.

She and Matt had come here after the last of the wolves had been transported. It was a beautiful place, a place to dream dreams . . . a place to find love.

And she had.

By the time she returned home, amethyst shadows dimpled the ground. Hints of the coming fall had put a tang in the air. Heat still clung to the day, but the evening had cooled off.

A patchy layer of clouds had sealed over, erasing the hint of sunshine she'd glimpsed earlier, but the heaviness that had settled around her heart the last weeks had lifted.

After checking with Uncle Ray the following day,

she made an unscheduled trip to the reservation and arranged to bring back Sarah and four other children. Time spent with the children would go a long way to heal her wounded heart.

What had Matt said about her dream of turning her ranch into a full-time place for children with disabilities?

If you want something hard enough, you'll make it happen.

She wanted it.

You have to say it aloud.

Feeling foolish, she said the words. "I want to turn the ranch into a full-time place for children with disabilities." She repeated the words.

Something stirred inside of her, a quickening of excitement that made her believe she could make her dream come true. If it did, she'd have Matt to thank.

Chapter Eleven

Matt had taken a temporary leave of absence from
the Akela Foundation and made the trip to California.
He'd stabled Trapper with the rancher who had sold the
gelding to him in the first place.

Someone else would monitor the wolves. The
thought brought a pang, but he pushed it aside to focus
on bridging the gulf between himself and his father.

Knowing he wouldn't find his father at home even
though the sun had long since dipped behind the horizon, Matt went straight to the sprawling industrial complex that comprised McCall Industries.

Erskin McCall sat behind the massive walnut desk in
his office. A gleam lit his eyes at Matt's appearance,
only to extinguish a moment later. He had aged in the

last months. The lines that furrowed his forehead and fanned from his eyes had deepened.

Matt acknowledged that he bore at least part of the blame. Regret twisted inside of him. "Are you sick?" he asked in quick concern.

Father and son had little in common, but Matt loved his parent. In many ways they were strangers, but the bond that existed between father and son was still there.

"Not in the way you mean." Erskin gave a short laugh.

"What's wrong?" Matt asked cautiously. Heart-to-hearts with his father wasn't something he had much experience with. He felt as though he were walking through a mire of quicksand.

Father gave son a measuring look. "Do you care?"

Matt stifled the surge of anger, realizing he hadn't given his parent much reason to believe otherwise. "I care." And knew that he had spoken the truth.

"I've done some soul-searching since you took off. Didn't much like what I saw." Erskin seemed beaten down, his eyes listless, broad shoulders stooped.

"What was that?" Matt asked cautiously.

"I saw a self-centered man who drove away everyone who had ever tried to love him."

Matt had no answer to that. Still, he sought for words of comfort. "You did the best you could."

Erskin shook his head. "You've always been straight with me. Don't start pussyfooting around the truth now."

To Matt's surprise, his father laughed—a gruff, rusty sound as though his throat muscles were unaccustomed to being used in such a way. "I've made a lot of mistakes. Especially where you're concerned. You were right about my cutting corners. I guess that's what made me so darn mad." He looked at Matt, his eyes holding a glint of affection which had been absent only moments ago. "I knew you were right, but I was too proud, too bullheaded, to admit it."

Matt stared at his father in surprise. He'd never heard Erskin McCall admit fault for anything.

"It runs in the family," Matt said, and recalled how Rebecca had accused him of misplaced pride.

"We've made some changes around here," Erskin said in an uncharacteristically hesitant voice. "If you stick around, you might like what you see."

For the first time in years, father and son looked at each other with something akin to respect.

"Are you happy in your new life?" his father asked unexpectedly.

"I was," Matt said. The phrasing stopped him. He *had* been happy with Rebecca.

He had a flash of memory, an image of Rebecca fighting the river and the cold to pull him to safety. His heart bumped in his chest.

As though aware of how much they'd revealed in the last minutes, both pulled back into themselves. The conversation veered to safer channels.

To his surprise, Matt discovered he and his father

saw eye to eye on more subjects than he'd believed possible. They both liked jazz, both were fiercely patriotic, and neither had the patience for golf. Small things in and of themselves, but they paved the way for future sharing.

At his father's invitation, Matt stayed at the house where he'd grown up. He had never thought of it as home. Now he looked at the stately mansion through new eyes.

Pictures of Matt from early childhood through college lined a wall in his father's den. How had he never noticed them before? An award for his scholarship to the university was framed and hung on the wall above his father's desk. Was that a picture of Matt's high school team occupying a corner of the desk?

He wondered now at his own blindness. All this time he'd believed his father hadn't cared. The pictures told a different story.

If he had been wrong about that, could he be wrong about other things as well? Could he be wrong about his own ability to sustain a relationship?

Inevitably, that brought him back to Rebecca. Random sparks of memory shot through him, and he knew he was far from forgetting her. Missing her was like a fire in his gut.

He realized that he had placed his bitter memories between himself and life and then used them as a shield to protect himself from involvement, but even that safeguard hadn't been enough.

"Your mother and I made mistakes," Erskin said unexpectedly. "Too many. I know you blamed her for walking out. I let you. The truth is, it was as much my fault as hers. Maybe more.

"I figured it was only a matter of time before you did too. I guess I wanted to push you away before you left."

So much made sense now. Matt stifled a sigh. So much time wasted.

What had Rebecca said about waste? That he was wasting the present on the past.

He couldn't forget the sight of her stricken face when he'd told her good-bye. He remembered the trembling of her lips, the tense way she'd held her hands, the pain in her eyes, and knew it was because of him.

His unhappy meanderings didn't allow for much sleep, but by the following morning, he had forced thoughts of Rebecca from his mind and was determined to focus on the present.

During the next week, father and son took cautious steps to a new relationship. Matt knew they'd never see eye to eye on many things, but they had reached an understanding, and he was grateful for that.

They toured the plant, and Matt saw that his father had told the truth about the new procedures. These first steps to a new relationship with his father brought Matt a peace he'd never before known.

If only he could find the same peace with his own thoughts. Memories of Rebecca continued to fill his mind and his heart. It didn't take much to have him remembering how her hair smelled, how her lips tasted, how soft her cheek felt against his cupped palm.

Matt scrubbed a hand along his jaw, wondering how he was going to make it through the rest of the day. He didn't dare think about tomorrow or all the tomorrows after that.

In a moment of revelation, he understood that he had clung to the painful ties to his past as though they were a security blanket.

The bitterness he'd carried with him for twenty-five years was gone, along with the pain. Instead he felt only a quiet acceptance. His mother wasn't an evil person. She just hadn't been cut out to be a mother. Why hadn't he understood that before?

Oh, he'd known it in his head, but his heart had never been able to accept it. For too many years he'd wrestled with the pain.

Why was he able to let go of it now? He searched for an answer.

Rebecca.

He and Erskin spent more time together in the next two weeks than they had in the last ten years.

They discussed his father's plans for the company. More importantly, they shared dreams, the intangibles which they'd never before put voice to.

Matt's last evening was spent at home. Over dinner, Erskin asked about Matt's plans.

He had postponed telling his father that he planned to return to Colorado.

"The two of us make a good team," Erskin said.

Matt hated to extinguish the hope in his father's eyes. The too-long silence hummed between them.

Erskin was the first to break it. "I think I knew you wouldn't be staying from that first night," he said. "You've got some unfinished business waiting for you back in Colorado." He paused, his lips lifting into a smile. "When you get it scttlcd, bring her back here. I'd like to meet her."

Matt wondered how his father knew that he'd left a woman behind. He started to ask, then stopped when Erskin's smile broadened to a full-fledged grin.

"I remember what it's like to be in love. She must be a special lady."

"She is. I love her. I'm going to ask her to marry me." A ghost of a laugh escaped him at the words.

They came with such ease that he wondered how he hadn't realized it before. He hadn't intended to say them, but there they were, hovering in the air, a stark admission of his feelings.

He loved Rebecca. Of course. That's why he'd fought so long and hard against his attraction to her. That's why he'd failed to understand what he was feeling. Love had been so lacking in his life that he didn't recognize it even when it was staring him in the face.

He'd never used the word *marriage* before. It occurred to him that since he'd met Rebecca, he had been thinking more and more of the future and less and less about the past.

She was the woman with whom he could picture spending the rest of his life. *There'd be children*, he thought. *Little boys and girls with dark hair and golden skin.*

"Bring her with you," Erskin repeated. "Soon."

For the first time in years, the two men hugged—an awkward clasping of shoulders that grew into a genuine embrace.

Matt felt the lifting of a great burden. Without the walls he'd erected around himself, he felt freer than he had in years.

Happiness awaited him. All he had to do was to reach out and take it. That and convince Rebecca that he loved her.

The question was whether he deserved her, whether he dared take the chance to find out. Answers which had deluded him only days ago now seemed clear.

Rebecca loved him and he loved her. Together they could make something good.

In her he'd found what had been missing in his own life. The love that comes from knowing another's heart as well as he knew his own. The love that keeps you going when all else has failed. The love that gives meaning to the quiet moments and meaning to others.

He only prayed he could find the words to tell her what was in his heart. All he had to do was convince her to give him a second chance.

Lately, he'd begun to think of home as wherever Rebecca was.

Dreams.

Rebecca.

The two went together.

Rebecca believed in dreams. She also had grit, courage, and a determination to find answers. Look at how she'd found a way for the ranchers and the wolves to co-exist. No matter that it had taken part of her land. She hadn't given the cost to herself a thought, had only wanted to save the animals and to protect the ranchers.

With the promise to return soon, Matt said good-bye to his father.

Matt made the trip to Colorado, rented a car, and headed to Miracle. An unfamiliar sense of anticipation hummed through him, a feeling of possibilities. A conversation with Uncle Ray netted him the information that Rebecca had gone riding.

Uncle Ray regarded Matt with grave intensity. "Have you found the truth you were seeking?"

"Yes. In Rebecca."

The old man nodded, apparently satisfied with the answer. "Then you will know where to find her."

It took Matt only a moment to understand Ray's meaning. He borrowed a horse from Ray and started out.

He found her there on the crest of the ridge overlooking the canyon where the wolves now resided. He remembered the first time she'd taken him there. She'd been beautiful that morning, her face flushed from excitement, her hair a ribbon of black under the sun.

Her head bent, she was a lonely figure, silhouetted

against the darkening sky. He lifted his gaze to study the gathering clouds. It was going to storm.

He dismounted and hobbled the horse. Within a few minutes he was only yards away from her. She couldn't have missed the sound of his approach. Still she didn't turn, until he uttered her name.

He wanted to tell her what was in his heart, needing her to know that she was his true love and that she had saved him. But nothing came out of his mouth but her name.

"Rebecca."

Did he move first, or did she? It didn't matter. Within moments, they were but a scant inch apart.

Each halted.

Each waited.

Each wondered what to say.

There was silence for the space of one breath. Then two. Three.

Matt ran his hands over her hair, her face, her shoulders, as if to reassure himself that she was, indeed, real.

"How did you know I was here?" she asked, her voice velvet dark in the desert twilight.

"I took a chance."

"Why?"

"Why what?" He was stalling, looking at her eyes for a hint of what she felt. What if she told him to take a flying leap? What if she had stopped loving him?

"Why did you come back?"

The time had come. "I love you. Part of me has from

the first time I saw you. The rest of me had to grow up enough to see it." There, he'd said it. The words he believed he'd never be able to say, much less mean, rushed from his lips.

He waited. More depended upon her answer than he wanted to admit, and he thought about the enormity of what he was about to do.

Responsibility.

Permanence.

Devotion.

At one time, the words would have terrified him, sent him running in the other direction as fast as his legs could carry him.

Now they thrilled him on a level deeper than he'd ever expected he was capable of. He opened his arms.

She walked into them, melted into his embrace.

He lowered his head until his lips waited a breath from hers. He was waiting, he realized, for a signal from her.

In answer, she raised her head enough that her lips found his, warm and tender. The kiss kindled a spiral of pleasure deep within him.

"You were right," he said when he lifted his head. "I was running. It feels like I've been running forever. Until you. I love you," he said again. He still marveled at the words. He'd shunned them, afraid of what they'd mean if he dared utter them aloud. Now they fell off his tongue with an ease that amazed him.

"I've been doing a lot of thinking. There're no guarantees. No absolutes. Except one."

"What's that?"

"This." He pressed another kiss to her lips. "I love you. Whatever happens, that won't change. It won't ever change."

She looked at him, her gaze searching his face. What she saw in his face must have given her the answer she sought, for at last, she smiled.

Her smile made his heart feel too big for his chest. The familiar expression tugged at him. He wanted her smiles. For the rest of his life, he wanted the warmth he saw there. "That's what I've been trying to tell you."

"What made you change your mind?"

"It wasn't a question of changing my mind. It was . . ." He paused, wanting her to understand what he'd only begun to. "I was afraid."

"Of me?"

"Of loving you." He drew a deep breath. "Of loving anyone. I kept remembering my parents. They loved each other. Once. But it died and left something ugly and bitter in its place. For a long time, too long, I couldn't see beyond that."

"Your mother didn't know what she was giving up. It wasn't your fault. It wasn't your fault," she repeated, her voice soft.

"I know that. Now." He cupped her face in his palms. "You helped me see the truth."

She shook her head. "I didn't do anything."

He put a finger to her lips. "You loved me. Even when I tried to push you away, you kept right on loving me."

She laughed softly. "I didn't have any choice in the matter."

His heart was full to overflowing. Her words ran through his mind, and all he could was to hold her. The softness of her skin, the tenderness of her touch, even the laughter she had saved for him, were nearly more than he could bear.

He kissed her.

They met as equals. Rebecca matched him kiss for kiss, strength for strength. Her world, which had been off-kilter for the last weeks, suddenly righted itself.

When she could breathe once more, she lifted his hand to her lips and skimmed a kiss across his knuckles. "We're not your parents."

"You're right."

"We're us—you and me."

"Can you forgive me for being a pig-headed fool?"

"What do you think?" she asked, and kissed him again. "What made you look for me here?"

"I remembered how much you loved the wolves. I took a chance you'd be here." The husky note in his voice told her how moved he was. "The first time I came here, it was with a woman. A very special woman. A woman who cared about what happened to the wolves even when she pretended to despise them."

"And you almost let her go," she said with a teasing smile.

Matt didn't return it. "I was a fool."

She shook her head. "Never that."

"I was a fool to let you go. I was going to convince you to forgive me even if it took the rest of my life. I'm glad it's not going to take that long."

"Not half as glad as I am." Tears stung her eyes at the words, sweet tears that dampened her cheeks. Dreams really did come true . . . and knights in shining armor did exist.

The darkening sky enfolded them, the stars sparkling like bangles against a sky of black velvet.

"Are you crying?" Matt asked.

"I always cry when I'm this happy."

"Does this mean you're going to cry at our wedding?"

Her thoughts scattered like sunbeams caught in the breeze. "Wedding?"

"As soon as you can arrange it." He gave her a hopeful look. "How about tomorrow?"

"You're crazy." And she loved him for it.

"You mean you're going to make me wait?"

A bubble of laughter spilled over. "Just a month." Love, sweet and so very right, filled her, so much so that she was afraid to believe it was real.

"It's real, all right," he said when she shared her thoughts. He fitted a finger beneath her chin. "I know I'm not a very good risk, but I'll do everything I can to make you happy."

"I know."

"You won't be sorry."

"I know that too."

"I love you."

"And I love you." Together, she thought, they'd make a family. One filled with love and laughter and dreams and hopes. There'd be tears as well. They would only make the love shine that much brighter.

"I've been thinking about your plan to turn the ranch into a full-time place for children with disabilities," he said unexpectedly. "Have you ever thought of taking on a partner?"

"It'd be great. The problem is no one would be willing to work for what I can afford to pay."

"I wouldn't be so sure about that. It ought to be someone who shares your dream. Someone to work toward it with you. Someone who can help with the kids and the horses."

She was beginning to understand. "Did you have someone in mind?"

"As a matter of fact, I do. Me."

"You'd do that?"

"In a heartbeat."

"But your job . . . I can't ask you to give it up."

"I can work right here. The Foundation is looking to hire someone to oversee the relocation on a part-time basis." He paused to take a breath. "There's more. With our two properties together, we can expand, run a bigger operation. I can help with the day-to-day stuff and give you more time to work with the kids." He framed her face with his hands. "I want to help make your dream come true. If you'll let me."

She looked at him, afraid to believe what she was hearing, but the love she saw shining in his eyes confirmed that she'd heard correctly.

"Our dream," she corrected softly. "Yours and mine." She laid his palm against his cheek.

"We'll make it come true. Anything's possible . . . as long as we're together."

Energy streamed through her. With Matt at her side, she could do anything. She covered his hand with her own.

"Together."